MW00937170

DRAGON TRIALS

RETURN OF THE DARKENING

BOOK ONE

AVA RICHARDSON

This is a work of fiction. Names, characters, places and incidents either are the product of imagination or are used fictitiously. Any resemblance to actual persons, living or dead, events or locales, is entirely coincidental.

RELAY PUBLISHING EDITION, February 2017

Copyright © 2017 Relay Publishing Ltd.

All rights reserved. Published in the United Kingdom by Relay Publishing.

No part of this book may be reproduced, published, distributed, displayed, performed, copied or stored for public or private use in any information retrieval system, or transmitted in any form by any mechanical, photographic or electronic process, including electronically or digitally on the Internet or World Wide Web, or over any network, or local area network, without written permission of the author.

Cover Art by Joemel Requeza

www.relaypub.com

BLURB

High-born Agathea Flamma intends to bring honor to her family by following in her brothers' footsteps and taking her rightful place as a Dragon Rider. With her only other option being marriage, Thea will not accept failure. She's not thrilled at her awkward, scruffy partner, Seb, but their dragon has chosen, and now the unlikely duo must learn to work as a team.

Seventeen-year-old Sebastian has long been ashamed of his drunken father and poor upbringing, but then he's chosen to train as a Dragon Rider at the prestigious Dragon Academy. Thrust into a world where he doesn't fit in, Seb finds a connection with his dragon that is even more powerful than he imagined. Soon, he's doing all he can to succeed and not embarrass his new partner, Thea.

When Seb hears rumors that an old danger is re-emerging, he and Thea begin to investigate. Armed only with their determination and the dragon they both ride, Thea and Seb may be the only defence against the Darkening that threatens to sweep over the land. Together, they will have to learn to work together to save their kingdom…or die trying.

Thank you for purchasing 'Dragons of Trials'

(Return of the Darkening Trilogy Book One)

If you would like to hear more about what I am up to, or continue to follow the stories set in this world with these characters—then please sign up for my mailing list at

http://www.subscribepage.com/b7o3io

You can also find me on me on

Facebook: www.facebook.com/AvaRichardsonBooks/

Homepage: www.AvaRichardsonBooks.com

TABLE OF CONTENTS

CHAPTER 1

THE CHOOSING

Every fifth year, the skies over the city of Torvald darken as large shadows swoop over the city, dark wingbeats blowing open window shutters and their bird-like cries disturbing babes and sleeping animals alike.

The city folk of Torvald are prepared for this ritual however, as the great Dragon Horns—the long brass instruments stationed along the top towers of the dragon enclosure—are blown on those mornings. Farmers and market folk rush to guide their skittish cattle out of sight, whilst children flock to the narrow cobbled streets or crowd atop the flat rooftops.

Choosing Day is a time of great celebration, excitement and anticipation for Torvald. It is the time that the great enclosure is unbarred and the young dragonets are released into the sky to choose their riders from amongst the humans below. It is a day that could forever change your fortunes; if you are brave and lucky enough. It is a day that heroes are made, and the future of the realm is secured.

*　　*　　*

"Dobbett, no! Get down from there right now." Dobbett was a

land-pig, although she looked somewhere between a short-snouted dog and a white fluffy cushion. She grunted nervously as she turned around and around atop the table, whimpering and grunting.

She always got like this. I wasn't very old the last time that Choosing Day came around; I must have been about thirteen or fourteen or so, but I remember how my little pet ran around my rooms, knocking everything off stands or dismantling shelves. I couldn't blame her: land-pigs are the natural food of dragons, and if she even caught a whiff of one, she went into a panic.

"No one's going to eat you, silly," I said to her in a stern voice, making sure I picked her up gently and set her down on the floor where her tiny claws immediately clacked on the tiles as she scampered under my bed.

Good Grief! I found myself smiling at her antics, despite myself. Dobbett was a welcome relief to the butterflies I was feeling in my stomach.

Today was Choosing Day, and that meant that today would be my last chance. If I wasn't picked now, then by the time another five years rolled by, Father would probably have married me off to some annoying, terribly fat merchant or nobleman.

Memories of the prince's last Winter Ball flashed through my mind, filling me at once with the most curious mixture of disgust and hopelessness. The prince, and all the royal family, had been there of course, and my older brothers too—Reynalt and Ryan—looking splendid in their dragon scale jerkins.

They managed to do it, I thought. *They got their own dragon.* My two older brothers were chosen almost as soon as they were old enough to sit on the saddle—even though it is always the dragon itself that does the choosing.

"As close as egg and mother, is a Flamma to a dragon," I mouthed the well-known Torvald saying desperately hoping it would prove true. I wanted to declare: I am Agathea Flamma, or more properly, *Lady* Agathea Flamma. Our household had sired Dragon Riders for the last hundred years, and the rooms of Flamma Hall were filled with the statues, busts and paintings of my great-uncles and grandfathers and great-great grandfathers who rode the mighty drakes into battle in defense of the city and the realm.

My brothers were chosen, why not me? Everyone had expected them to be chosen. No one expected me to be.

I am a girl. They say I am better suited to marrying well, running an estate, raising little Dragon Riders all of my own... "Ugh!" I snorted in disgust, throwing open the patio doors to the balcony of the tower and walking out into the fresh morning air.

The last of the Dragon Horns just finished their mournful cry. I could already hear cries and screams of excitement as the shapes flew out of Mount Hammal, the dragon enclosure far over the mountain from here. They looked so beautiful. Long, sinuous necks, powerful; each one a different colour. Today there are green, blue, black—even a red.

They swooped and soared over the city, skimming over its rooftops and around the many terraces to the cheers and cries of the people below. I saw some people trying to entice the dragons to choose them by waving colourful flags or roasting land-pigs right on their rooftops.

Not for these beasts, however. These great ones were reveling in their freedom: performing barrel rolls and turns in the air, one after another. Then some smell would catch their nose and they followed the scent like a lightning flash to their chosen rider.

No one really knows why or how the great wyrms chose their two riders. Some say it's magic, others say that dragons can read your soul, so they choose the ones that they know they can live and work with the best. You have to have two riders for every dragon though: a navigator and a protector. The navigator is like the pilot and the guide; some say they can almost sense their dragon's emotions. The protector is the one who gets to fire arrows, throw lances and use swords to defend both dragon and the navigator when they are on patrols.

Not that Torvald had gotten into any wars over the last hundred years. The fact that we had the dragons—or should that be the other way around?—meant our enemies rapidly sued for peace. We still have trouble with bandits and cattle rustlers of course—last summer all it took for my brothers to scare them off was one low fly-by. There has always been one threat, however—that of the Darkening returning.

My father swore the old stories were true, but my mother did not like to hear him speak of those tales. I have only heard the old legends once. My father's stories left me with such nightmares—where I dreamed of being claimed by darkness, where I was lost in a deep blackness—that it left me unable to do more than curl into a shivering ball and cry.

I have forgotten most of the old tales, but I still remember the fear they left in my bones. My brothers told me they are just stories to make children behave, but I wonder at times if they are right, for we still have Dragon Riders patrolling against the return of the Darkening.

What would Father think if I was actually chosen to be a rider? I scanned the horizon, searching for the dragons. *Where are they? Have all the riders already been chosen? Is my chance over?* It couldn't be. It just couldn't. I imagined the look on my father's face if he heard the news. He would be delighted, surely, that all his children had been chosen. It would make the Flamma House a force really to be reckoned with.

And I just want to make my father proud of me. I realize this, running to the balcony and turning around, hearing the telltale caw of the giant lizards; not being able to see them yet.

He wants me to get married, another part of my mind kept thinking. *He wants me to 'do the right thing' and bring some respectability to our family.*

"I can't do it," I whisper, shutting my eyes tight against tears threatening to spill over my lashes.

There was a breath of fresh air against my face and my hair lifted. A round of cheers and shouts rose up from the city below. I felt heartbroken. The last dragon must have made its choice—and it wasn't me.

Suddenly, it went dark. I opened my eyes—and almost fainted.

A red wyrm slowly descended to our tower. It was young, its forehead horns barely as big as my hand at the moment, but in fine shape. And a red, too. I knew they were fierce and rare. The wyrm made a twittering noise in the back of its throat. I could see its throat expanding and contracting like a bellows as it raised its wings to catch the thermals and hang in the air. Its eyes were a brilliant green-gold, a colour I had never seen before. It was holding me in its steady gaze. Now I could really understand why everyone thought they had the power to hypnotize.

Its great head with an elongated snout was still, almost calm, as it lowered its claws to grab onto the side of the tower, splintering rock and the wooden windowsill as it did so. Half of its bulk was atop the tower and the other half gently lowered onto the wide, semi-circular balcony beside me.

"Uh…h-hi?" I said, feeling a rush of panic as the beast slipped a forked tongue into the air, tasting its choice. All thought of the correct etiquette went out of my head as I stared into its great, golden-green eyes.

I got the incredible sensation this young beast was smirking at me as it tasted the air again and *huffed* gently into the space above my head. Breath smelling like wood-smoke mixed with something aromatic, like basil or pepper.

"Dear…dear dragon, my name is Agathea Flamma, of the H-House Flamma, and I th-thank you…" I tried to stammer through the traditional greeting that every child in Torvald learned by the time they were ten.

The beast nudged its head forward, slowly inclining it until it was just a foot away from me. I stretched out my hand, feeling a curious heat radiating from its scales. It was so shiny and new. The only other dragons I had seen were the ones that my brothers or the prince rode; they were much older, with scales that had lost some of their luster or become cracked, scratched and broken with time.

Incredibly, and I could hardly breathe, the creature bumped its head against my hand. Despite the heat radiating from its breath, the scales felt cool and smooth to my touch. Not cold, but not blistering hot either. Like a cool lake on a hot summer day.

"I-I," I tried to speak, finding myself unable to gather my thoughts or articulate just what I was feeling. *Me. A Dragon Rider. I'll be one of the very few women riders in the whole service.*

Before I could concentrate my thoughts, there was a buffet of strong air almost knocking me off of my feet and the dragon was in the air. *Am I wrong?* I thought for a moment the dragon must have made a mistake—maybe it had been sensing my older brothers and became confused.

But then the tower dropped away. I was yanked upward with a wail. The dragon had lightly clasped me in its two, warm-and-cool talons and I was being carried through the air like a precious prize, back to Mount Hammal and the dragon enclosure.

CHAPTER 2

THE WRONG BOY

I heard the Dragon Horns blowing on the morning of the Choosing, just like everyone else. However, unlike everyone else, I was already up and awake, well into my fourth or fifth hour of the day.

That's what it is like as a blacksmith's boy. There's always ingots to be hauled in, bellows to be primed, wood to be chopped and the foundries to be cleaned. My da is the blacksmith for Monger's Lane, and I have to be up before the crack of dawn to make sure the forge is ready when he starts work.

Which probably won't be until mid-day if he was out at the inn again last night. A twinge of embarrassment and shame warmed my face. My father liked his flagon of ale at the end of a working day. He also seemed to like it in the evening and halfway through the night as well.

Stop that, Sebastian, I chided myself. It's not right to think ill of your father no matter how much he drinks! I didn't mind the work. It felt good to be up early and to get everything ready for the other apprentices and junior smiths. I even made time to chop some wood for Old Widow Hu a few doors down. I always tried to do what I could for her because the poor woman was nearly blind, needing all the help she could get.

But the dragons—I loved to see the dragons. All of my short seventeen years I had been dreaming of them—the freedom they knew of flying through the air, above the world and all its troubles, the power of every muscle, the strength of every wiry sinew. They are such beautiful creatures. They offered the steady loyalty, strength and wisdom of a horse, but with the playfulness, speed, and sometimes the temperament, of a cat.

Sometimes we work on the rider's tack, which was such an honor, but sadly that didn't happen often enough to please me. The Dragon Riders of Torvald usually got their kit remade and polished at one of the bigger, throne-endorsed smithies. But every now and again, a few small buckles or harness clips filtered down our way to be seen to.

I would hold them in my hand, imagining which part of a rider's kit they corresponded to, taking care to re-tool the fine designs etched into their surface, polishing and polishing until they gleamed as good as new. It was one of the few paid jobs that my da let me do by myself, knowing I would put the extra work in just because I loved dragons.

I'd seen a flash of one last year. A brilliant scintillating flash of blue and green that soared over Monger's Lane. It moved as fast as a hawk. For a moment, I swore I had looked up past the towering, crowded houses of the street down here and had seen it looking down at me with eyes like the golden-green of a summer lake or the first flush of spring leaves. No one believed me of course. They said I was imagining it. That dragons only had eyes and noses for their riders, but it had happened. I knew it had. I'll never forget it.

This morning, I was working extra hard trying to clear my duties for the day, hoping I might get to finish early enough to see the last few choices of the day. Everyone would talk about the choices for the next five years. How this blue dragon or that white wyrm approached their rider. Did they go on foot? Did they snatch them from their windows?

I moved the final barrow of split logs, seeing a whole collection of end-pieces, scrappy tops and tree-hearts left. It would be too much work to break them down and feed them into the kilns. Besides, they would give an uneven burn, so I loaded them onto a wheelbarrow and decided to take them to Old Widow Hu. She would be pleased for the free firewood, and da couldn't do anything with them anyway.

Monger's Lane was a tight little community, more than just a lane really, but not much bigger than one. The poorest district in the city, with people living in makeshift houses next to each other, cheek by jowl, my ma said. I knew it wasn't much, but I liked living here. The people were honest. Old Widow Hu had a hovel poorer than most, a collection of mud and brick walls and wooden beams almost leaning against the stronger houses next door. As I neared her home, in the background I could hear the cheers and gasps as the dragons must have swooped overhead. I knocked on her oddly-fitting wooden door and waited as a breeze blew down the alley behind me.

It took a little while for Old Widow Hu to answer her door, but I didn't mind. When she did, she peered past me and blinked, then looked at my barrel. "Oh, thank you Sebastian, but you've already done me such a kindness," she was saying in a cracked and croaking voice.

"These are free, ma'am. I'd like to think someone might take care of my step-mam if ever she got older and had no one around." I heaved the wood onto the pile by the side of her door. I was forced to jump back immediately as a few of the tiles fell off her roof above us.

"Oh, dear goodness!" Old Widow Hu was looking up at me.

She must not be able see me, I thought. "It's okay, Mrs. Hu. It's just me, Sebastian."

"N-no, Seb…" her voice quavered. "I think there's someone to see you." She hurriedly stepped back into her hovel.

Oh no. It must be Father. He must be annoyed at me for something.

I turned and came face to face with the long, sinuous, muscular neck and the strong snout of a red dragon. It had golden-green eyes, eyes the colour of the sun glinting off polished gold or seen through the leaves of a beech forest at mid-day. She was beautiful.

How do I know it's a she? I thought, but I knew. I just knew.

She didn't look like a dragon to me. She looked—she just looked like herself. Not a thing, not a lizard or a beast. I could feel something stirring in my breast, my heart thumping and a lump in my throat as I raised a hand up to her. She put her snout on the edge of my fingers, letting me touch the sensitive mouth that I knew surrounded her teeth and then huffed a warm breath of pine smoke and coal-dust over me, fluffing my thatch of hair.

You're playing with me, aren't you? I smiled, blowing air back onto her snout.

With a sudden sneeze, the dragon shook its head and made a chirruping noise, oddly musical, like a bird.

"Seb! Seb! What are you doing?" a voice shouted, alarmed and fearful—my da, his drunken gait exaggerated by the alarm and anger in his voice.

The dragon then did something I had been hoping for all my life, but never expecting. It seized me with its front feet, black talons the length of my whole forearm curling gently against me and not even hurting a tiny bit, and launched itself into the air.

"You've got the wrong boy!" I heard my father yell, along

with the Old Widow Hu's reply, "no, I think that it's got just the right one!"

CHAPTER 3

THE DRAGON ACADEMY

The spire of Hammal Mountain, called Mount Hammal, rose up in front of us. Everyone is going to be so jealous of me. My brothers would be because I had been chosen by a red; my father because he had never been chosen, and all my friends would stare because I would be one of the few female riders. The only other girl at the academy, a girl named Varla, was about Ryan's age, but hadn't graduated yet.

Being held in the dragon's claws was terrifying. Not that it hurt me—it didn't hurt at all, but I could feel the cold air whipping around, over my breeches and long jerkin. I wish I'd dressed properly for this. I kept thinking of my light cream trousers and the embroidered-green tunic-jerkin I could even now be wearing. The green would work brilliantly with the dragon's red.

I had never been to the academy of course, but I had heard all about it from Reynalt and Ryan. They both talked about it like it was a drag and a bore, but I could tell how secretly proud they were of going here.

The whole city of Torvald was built around the body of Mount Hammal, extending in crowded terraces up the mountain which was a giant, old volcano. The central crater had been topped with high walls that gleamed when the sun set. This was the dragon enclosure where the dragons lived and slept. The academy where they trained the riders sat alongside the enclosure, its towers abutting the gleaming, pale wall. The Dragon Academy extended along the narrow ridge like a picture of one of those far-away, mountain monasteries.

We flew over a scattering of ancient oak trees that were larger than any house. The trees grew larger as the dragon skimmed the air toward one of the large wooden platforms affixed to the side of the academy.

"Easy now. Easy," I said, a little panicked as we rushed toward the rounded wooden boards with one small red flay affixed to its edge. I could see other chosen trainee riders and the academy staff with their tell-tale horned helmets, knee and elbow bracers. The dragon shrieked like an eagle, depositing me gently on the platform with only a meter or so for me to fall. I rolled out of the short fall to be caught by someone.

"Hey!" I turned back to my red beast only to see it had already shifted and jumped from the platform, swooping down over the side of the mountain and back into the city; getting its second rider, no doubt.

"Are you okay?" A short, heavy-set boy with dark hair had caught me. He was one of the other trainees. I could tell that from his clothes, which were just a tunic and breeches, and not the gleaming armor of a Dragon Rider. He gave me a hand back up on my feet.

"Yeah—fine. Fine!" I stood and brushed myself off. I felt queasy and sick as I stood, excited to see who my fellow rider was going to be.

"Congratulations!" Other Dragon Riders, looking fine in their armor—the chest plates and armguards bright in the sun—were approaching, shouting and cheering the trainees selected. The wooden platforms opened onto a wide stone area that was the top of a thick wall. Looking around, I could see about a dozen trainees that had already been selected. They stood out because they didn't have armor or helmets and tunics of all colours fluttered in the breeze. The Dragon Riders in their glinting armor of metal and leather were climbing to the platforms on stone stairs and were welcoming friends or family to the academy, clapping the trainees on the back or hoisting them into the air. The crowd around me seemed particularly large, and I thought it might be because of my ruddy-golden hair, freckles and my slighter frame which gave away that I was a girl.

I heard a familiar laugh and looked over to see my brother Ryan. He came up to me and grabbed my shoulder. "You'd better get off the platform before your dragon comes back with your fellow rider!"

"Ryan, I did it!" I threw my arms around my older brother. He patted me awkwardly on the back.

"Well done, Sis, well done, but easy. I've got a reputation to keep." He pulled my arms away, and led the way to the stone palisade wall where I could watch for the return of the red.

"Your dragon is the last to come back in," Ryan said. "It'll be the talk of the academy, your red picking a girl of all things."

"It'll be the talk of the city," said another boy. He was with the stocky kid who had helped me up. With his slicked-back, black hair and his blue shirt and breeches, I knew him at once. He was from House Veer, a family with a history of riders almost as good as House Flamma.

"Beris." I gave him a nod. His family was mostly chosen by blues, so that was why he'd dressed the way he had. I'd known him since childhood for all the noble Houses of Torvald studied together and met up regularly at the king's banquets and balls. We had all trained together.

"I shouldn't be surprised that we've got another Flamma up here," he drawled the words with a twist to his mouth. He was trying to sound joking, but I caught the edge of something else in his tone. He had never liked sparring with me and I knew he thought it was beneath him to have to fight with a girl.

I punched him in the arm for the jibe and put some muscle

behind my fist. "Just shows my red has taste, that's all." I couldn't help grinning. I'd been chosen and I didn't care who knew it.

Since the dragons only choose every five years, the academy only took in new trainees every five years, too. At twenty-four, Ryan was five years older than I, and Reynalt five years older than him. With ten years in the saddle, Reynalt was considered an experienced Dragon Rider. He had graduated faster than any other trainee, and both he and Ryan had become full Dragon Riders by coming out of the academy with honors. But while Reynalt was one of the best Dragon Riders in Torvald, it was Ryan to whom most people deferred—he just had an air of a leader about him. Beris and two other trainees that I knew—Shakasta and Syl—did that now, tipping their heads and stepping back. Ryan had been chosen along with Prince Justin, the only son of King Durance Torvald by the same dragon, and so my brother was the navigator to the prince's protector position on a green drake.

"Shakasta, Syl." I nodded to the others, the guys I'd be training with. For once, I felt as though I had a right to be here. My chest lifted with pride and I pulled in a deep breath.

I just hope that Father sees it the same way that I do. The crowd around me started to whistle and point to the sky. I turned to see my red making its way back to the academy from the city, its broad wings forcing it up the thermals in easy, strong strokes. I thought the red might grow into a strong, handsome beast, if treated right and fed well.

"Who's it got? Where is he?" Beris was saying, shading his eyes and trying to look at the dragon's clasped claws.

"I bet it's Fabian from House Trulo," said Shakasta. "He's excellent at horse riding."

Syl punched Shakasta's arm. "Horse riding is hardly the same as dragon riding, you dolt."

The red screeched and landed on the wooden platform, depositing its bundle in a tangle of legs and messy hair. Looking at him, I made to move forward to greet my friend, but then stopped. The figure that had landed and rolled was looking up in wonder at the dragon above him. He looked all elbows and knees. He was thin, messy-haired and grubby.

"He's not anyone I remember," Shakasta said and shifted uncomfortably on his feet.

"I'm sorry to say it, lads, but he looks a bit poor, don't you think?" Beris said under his breath. Only those standing near him could hear, but I heard.

My face heated. This was my other rider? Beris was totally right. The boy sitting with a look of naïve wonder on his mooncalf face looked pretty poor indeed. No finery. No house crest on his tunic. In fact, his tunic was full of holes and slashes of soot and ash streaked his face, his hands and his breeches.

"By the breath of the First Dragon, he hasn't even got any shoes on." Beris burst out into laughter, doubling over. Others started to chuckle.

Ryan stepped forward, his mouth set. "Let's not be unfair."

Face burning, I turned away. I felt so ashamed. How could the red do this to me? What was it thinking? It must have made the wrong choice. It just must have.

"Well, good luck, Thea." Beris was grinning like a fool. "He looks as though he hasn't seen a bar of soap in ages. You may have to wear a scarf over your face to ride with the likes of him."

"Thea…" Ryan said. I knew that warning tone of voice. He was about to offer one of his sage bits of advice that I always hated.

This is going to ruin everything. Everyone will think I won't be as good a rider because of this…this dirty rag. I knew I couldn't give in to humiliation. There was only one way to deal with this embarrassment. I was a Flamma and it was time I acted like it. Before Ryan could make me look weak in front of the others, I took a step forward to introduce myself to the boy. With my head held high, I gave him my best, most noble stance—the one I had learned from Mother when she addressed the king himself. Let them see a lady in action, someone who deserves to be here.

"Friend, I am Lady Agathea Flamma. It is a delight to meet you. This red chose us both." It wasn't a delight, and my voice wavered slightly at the start of that lie, but I hoped I was sounding confident and that I looked nonchalant when I offered him my hand to help him to his feet.

The boy, his ridiculous thatch of dark-brown hair sticking out everywhere, grinned widely, and blushed as red as the dragon's hide. "Wow, hey, hi—uh, it is a pleasure to meet you!" He shuffled his feet, his movements jerky, his excitement as clear as his nervousness. "You're a Flamma? Wow—I've heard all about your family, you're the best riders of them all."

He looked like he was fighting his own nervousness. He was clearly overawed by everything that was happening to him. He kept looking back up at the dragon, which was busy preening its wings elegantly.

"Uh, I'm Sebastian. Sebastian Smith," he stuck out his hand to shake my hand, something no noble would do, for we bowed to each other and nodded and never touched each other unless it was in sparring.

And he had just made me mad. How was he going to make a good Dragon Rider? He couldn't even greet another person correctly. How could I possibly trust this…this dirty boy in training or when we're out on patrol. He doesn't look like he's ever ridden anything except a chair.

I could see muscles through the tatters in his tunic. He was tall with long legs and arms, and a gap between his front teeth. He had dark brown eyes that matched his hair, but all I could think of were the smudges on his skin. He stank too, smelling of coal fire. I forced myself to smile through my teeth, but my heart sank. This was terrible. This was all terrible.

"Candidates," a loud, gruff voice barked. I turned, glad to look away from the boy my red had chosen to train with me. "I am Commander Hegarty and I will be your head instructor for the duration of your time here at the academy. Roll up and listen—the time flies quite literally up here."

I forced out a brittle smile. Standing next to the boy who smelled of fire and dirt, I knew he would probably be my undoing. Tears stung my eyes and I blinked them away, but I feared I was never going to become a fully-fledged Dragon Rider.

CHAPTER 4

AN INTRODUCTION TO DRAGONS

The room seemed filled with noble names—and a girl who stared at me as if I was dirt, which I was, in a way. All the others chosen by the dragons wore fine clothes, and had clean hands which looked as if they had seen little work. I knew I would not fit in with them. But I didn't care. A dragon had chosen me. I turned to stare at the commander who had called everyone to order.

This Commander Hegarty was a short man, but I could see immediately he had a wiry kind of strength. He led all the trainees down the stairs from the platform and into a huge, stone room at the base of one of the towers. Flags of all the noble families of Torvald—all past Dragon Riders—hung from the one of the thick wooden beams that held up the ceiling. The room had no furniture, but staffs and swords hung from the walls and thick, wooden planks covered the floor. I glanced around and tried to keep my mouth from falling open. I'd never seen such a huge room. So I tried to focus on the commander.

He looked a stocky-man much like some of the woodcutters did, who came into Torvald. Sort of like he'd never eaten very much, but everything he did eat got used up to make muscles. I respected that. This man wasn't like my da, with a podgy belly

24

and forearms the size of my head. Looking around the crowd of us with steel-grey eyes, he seemed to be taking us all in with a measuring stare. He gave a nod and I hoped that meant he approved all the choices. He looked every bit the military commander in an open-faced helmet with sweeping-back horns and a shirt of dull steel mail and sturdy canvas and leather trousers and boots. His face had a couple of white scars threatening the line of a thick moustache. I thought he seemed stronger than any of us who must be only a third of his age.

"Candidates, you have all had the good fortune to be chosen to be trained here on Hammal Mountain to become Dragon Riders. I'm sure most of you know what this means, but let me go over the basics for you."

He coughed and shifted, his leather not making a sound, which meant it was oiled, and his armor, the metal plates made to look like dragon scales, fit him like a second skin. "The Dragon Academy has been up on this mountain since the city of Torvald was just a keep on the slope of Dragon Mountain. It was once an ancient monastery for friends of the dragons—people who were attracted or drawn here because they wanted to get to know dragons, and the dragons wanted to get to know them. After a long, long time, some of those gathered here began to think about the future and they set up a community. Others flocked to their banners and so Torvald was born. The great noble houses—I see House Flamma and House Veer represented here—are the descendants of those first dragon friends."

Beside me, someone moved. I glanced over to see the girl—Agathea Flamma she'd called herself—smile proudly. She was a little thing, a head smaller than me, with bright red-gold hair that seemed to curl and pull itself from how she'd tried to tie it back. She looked slim and slight, and I wondered how it was that a dragon could possibly want her for a rider. But then, the dragon had chosen me too, so perhaps the dragon had seen something I could not see. I was glad for her, but it made me feel a little out of place to see all these nobles here. I wondered what it was like, how great it must be, to be able to say that you are part of a tradition that went back centuries. All I could say was that my father was a smith, and his father had been one, too. I knew nothing more of my family's history. But the commander was talking so I turned back to listen to him.

Arms crossed, he stared at the trainees, his gaze not unkind. "And so, the monastery turned into the Dragon Academy, to train those who would protect the city of Torvald and our realm. Here we train riders on how to work with their dragons, how to fly, how to read the landscape, how to attack, defend and signal to each other. As you know, the relationship between a dragon and its riders is a very special one." The commander scowled as he looked us over, and I was wondering if he thought our lack of experience a bad thing for he punched his words out as if to reinforce this point.

To me, it was obvious what he meant. How anyone could mistreat, or not feel in awe of, their dragon.

"As you know, it takes two riders to properly accompany a dragon. The rider sitting up near the neck is called the navigator—they help fly, direct and commune with the beast. The protector's saddle sits further back, behind the dragon's shoulders. They are the ones who must protect the dragon and the navigator, and the protector is the principle warrior whenever the dragon takes to the ground."

There was a murmur from the students around me. I could see a lot of them nodding as if all of this was old news to them, but I'd never known any of this.

"Commander?" this was from my very own partner, Thea. She looked splendid in a pale blue tunic that matched her eyes. With her golden hair, she looked a true noble, and she sounded confident and resolute as she spoke. Not like I would. Words tangled my tongue. I stumbled over them whenever I had tried to speak out loud in a group. And I knew what my clothes looked like—like they didn't fit me and had once been my father's. I wondered how I would actually be able to fit in with these others.

"Yes, Candidate Flamma?" the commander barked out the words.

"Will we get to work with the Tremain saddles, sir?" she asked, displaying just how much she knew about dragon riding already. I'd heard about these saddles, but only through secondhand reports from other smiths who had made minor repairs to them. They were a fancy dragon saddle that allowed the protectors and navigators to be much more maneuverable in the air. I didn't really know how they did that. I was just happy to be here at all.

"Ha. Points for being eager, trainee, but you'll only get some actual flying experience after the academy has put you all through your paces." The commander gave a firm nod. "Now, as I was saying, every dragon has two riders and those riders are chosen by the dragon itself. It can sense which humans it will be able to work with. Both of you, whichever is a navigator or a protector, are here because you have something—a trait, an aptitude, a way of approaching a problem—that the dragon recognizes in you. I cannot impress enough how it is your dragon that is the reason why you are here. Respect that choice."

The commander paused for a second as if to let that thought sink in. I shifted on my feet. This meant I should not question why I was here—my dragon had wanted me and that should be that. The commander's voice dropped lower. "That being said, your teachers will be testing you and watching you. Over the next two weeks we will have a routine of training and learning that will draw out your strengths and expose weaknesses. At the end of that time, there will be a test to see whether you are fit for protector or navigator material. You will both be expected to learn as much as you can about your dragon, about each other, about the different roles of each rider before the selection is made. Understood?"

"Aye, Commander." The voices rose up around me, one by one, going down the line of all the trainees who stood in this great hall. When it came to my turn, I gulped loudly before I could speak. My voice cracked. I could feel all eyes on me. My face heated, but I could see the commander was looking at me not unkindly. His gaze held on me steadily, like I was a young horse that he was about to shoe. Assessing me, measuring me, I thought. Wondering if I will be trouble.

After a second, he broke off his gaze. "You'll be staying at the academy, but every two months until you graduate or fail you can have a day to yourself, which you can spend in the city or visiting your family should you wish. However, I need not remind any of you that tardiness will never be tolerated. Nor will intoxication, fighting, bullying or any other manner of behavior not fitting a Dragon Rider of Torvald." He glowered sternly at everyone. "If you break any of our rules, even once, then you will have training and flying privileges revoked until we feel you have learned your lesson. If you break any of our rules more than once, you may expect harsh punishment. A third violation and you will say goodbye to your dragon, and your fellow rider will also be out. Your dragon will return to the enclosure. So…failure means you will be letting down not just yourself, but also the whole city of

Torvald, your family, your fellow rider and the dragon which chose you!" the commander glanced around the room. Silence held everyone—I couldn't even hear anyone breathing, but my heart thudded in my ears.

This wasn't just an opportunity for me, it was also a chance for my whole family to get out of Monger's Lane. If I did well, if I flew and proved myself, I might be able to make a real difference to the people of my home district. Dragon Riders were respected—and well-paid. And what would happen if the other poor kids could see that one of their own—a Monger's Lane brat with no shoes—had made it all the way to the top as a Dragon Rider? It would make such a difference.

The commander seemed to relax. He spread his booted feet wider and his moustache even twitched in an almost-smile. "For now, however, all of you will be free of duties until tomorrow morning when the real training begins. You may use your time to explore the academy, or go down into the city to pack what you need and return. I would urge all of you to say goodbye to your dragon before you leave."

"Goodbye?" my voice sounded startled and a bit strangled. What was the commander talking about? A sniggering sounded behind me, coming from some of the other students.

"Yes, trainee." The commander's voice was not quite so sword-stern as it had been. "This is the last time that you will be seeing your dragon for these first two weeks of training. The more experienced dragon handlers and riders will be preparing your beast, and you have to get used to working with your fellow rider. After two weeks, you will be presented to your dragon as a complete unit, making it much easier for your dragon to accept and follow you."

"Uh-oh. I see," I said, my face hot again and feeling stupid.

"Until tomorrow, trainees, your time is your own. Let me say one final thing—congratulations and welcome to the Dragon Academy of Hammal Mountain. May you make your families and your city proud."

A rousing cheer lifted from the other students. I started out of the hall with the others. I was wildly glad to be here, of course, but the thought was tinged with a sadness that we wouldn't actually get to be with our dragon for the first bit. She was so very lovely that I wanted nothing more than to stare at her for hours. Around me, the rest of the students seemed to be nudging each other and swapping congratulations. Out in the grounds, they pointed up at their dragons, still perched on the landing platforms. One of the trainees—a tall, thin boy— commented on another's dragon, saying that it looked wyrm-like, meaning round in the belly and heavy. I frowned at him. All dragons were beautiful, fierce and utterly amazing creatures.

One of the stockier boys with black hair called out, "Hey,

Thea? You coming down to the Troll's Head? A few of us are going down to celebrate. Last night of freedom, hey?"

I guessed the place must be some sort of tavern—a better one than any in Monger's Lane. Thea looked pleased to me, for she straightened and smiled. She was going to be included in their little gang, and I noticed she was standing a little way from me.

But she turned to me and frowned. "Uh—Sebastian? You want to come?" She didn't sound as if she wanted to make the offer. "We're going down to a tavern in the northern district of the city."

I waved to the landing platforms, one foot already on the bottom of the stone stairs that led upward. "Don't you want to hang out with our dragon? We've got to say goodbye to her, so I thought maybe we could spend the evening just, you know…hanging out with her. We won't get a chance to see her again for two weeks."

"Her?" Thea tipped her head to one side. "I thought fighting dragons were all drakes?"

I shook my head. Was not her gender obvious? But then again, how did I know with such certainty that she was a she? It just seemed obvious in the way she held her head, the look in her eyes as she regarded us, and how she spent time preening her wings rather than flapping them and pushing out her chest like some of the other dragons.

"No, she is definitely a she," I said, certain of it. "Come on, let's say goodbye at least." I grabbed Thea's wrist and dragged her up the stairs with me, ignoring how her eyes went wide and her mouth fell open.

At the top of the stairs, I stopped, breathless. Our red dragon gave a musical chirrup. She cocked her head to one side, and I knew she was interested in what we were doing. She unfolded a long neck, leaning forward to huff air over us, as if she was checking that we were the ones she had chosen.

"Don't worry, girl, it's us, Seb and Thea." I kept my voice low and smooth. Reaching out, I gave her nose a rub. Her chirruping turned into a deeper, almost throaty purr.

"Lady Dragon," Thea said beside me, her tone strained and careful. I turned to see her kneeling on the floor, head bowed. "I thank you from the bottom of my heart for choosing me and I hope I can serve you well." She looked up, and I saw real fervor and honesty in her eyes as she said, "I promise I will treat you well, just as all of House Flamma have treated their dragons with respect and honor."

I thought it a pretty speech, but also a bit weird. The dragon just wanted to get to know us, not see us bow and curtsey. I wondered what our dragon would do.

The red dragon paused, looked at Thea and very slowly, very gently, put her snout down in the air in front of Thea's earnest face. She gently rubbed the side of Thea's face with her own scaly snout.

"It means she says yes," I said, unthinking.

"I know what it means," Thea whispered. A chorus of choked laughter broke out behind us. I turned to see three other trainees—the ones who had asked Thea to go with them to a tavern—pulling faces about us getting so cozy with our dragon.

Standing, her face red, Thea ignored them. She gave another bow. "Thank you, Lady Dragon, thank you." Thea stood, brushed her knees off, and turned away in a quick motion. "I'm off to the pub, come or stay, I don't care." She threw the words at me, joining up with her friends and punching them on the shoulders to stop them laughing. They all started back down the stairs.

Disappointment gathered in my chest in a hard lump. Maybe I had done something wrong and I didn't even know what it was.

A gentle nudge on my shoulder bumped me from my mood. I turned to see the red dragon blinking at me with beautiful gold-green eyes. She chirruped again and pulled away quickly.

"What?" I said. Had I done something wrong with her as well?

The red chirruped again and her head bobbed up and down on her long neck.

I grinned. "Oh, you want me to play with you, do you?" It was then that I realized just how young she was. She was a little older than me, I saw, maybe about Thea's age in dragon terms.

She just wants friends. I did, too. Raising my hands, I pulled an exaggerated snarl and then ran toward her like I was a monster. The red chirruped excitedly, let out a small puff of flame and darted this way and that over the wooden platform in a game of chase. And I knew I had one friend—but a friend I would not see again for two weeks.

CHAPTER 5

AN INTRODUCTION TO BRUISES

"No, it's like…" I tried to find the words to explain what I meant, but the look on Seb's face only showed just how much he didn't get it.

"Across your body and then up." I demonstrated the move with my own practice wooden staff. It was actually a classic defensive move, one of the first you learned when you started any training. I had mastered it by the time I was twelve. Sebastian was seventeen, just a year younger than me, but he was a blacksmith's son. He had muscles and not much brain, or so it seemed. He should be able to perform one simple movement with a quarterstaff, but I was starting to wonder if he could do anything right.

Seb looked up at me from the floor, rubbing his elbow where a red welt was slowly appearing.

I sighed and pushed my hair out of eyes. It was coming out of the leather tie I used to keep it back, and I was starting to think about cutting it to be short the way all the boys wore theirs. "Look, it's okay. Come on, up you go." I reached down and helped Seb up before walking back to my starting mark and turning to begin the exercise again.

It had been almost a week now, and I had been training with Sebastian every day. We started with exercises, running over the trails on Mount Hammal in the morning, doing a bit of rock climbing, then swimming in the cold lakes that formed under the snow caps of the mountains. In the afternoons we had weapons training. Today, all the trainees—we were called scrubs, for we weren't even fit to scrub down a Dragon Rider's saddle—were working our way back and forth across the sandy practice floor of the open area between the towers of the academy, trading blows and attacking moves.

The other trainees were having a great time so far as I could tell. I could hear them laughing and talking. It was hard work, but nothing that was too far beyond our skills. Most of the others, like Beris, Shakasta and Syl, were from the noble Houses of Torvald. We'd all had our share of weapons training, paid for by the throne itself. Commoners weren't allowed to train with sword and staff. Commoners like Sebastian.

I turned to see he was standing near the white chalk starting point, totally oblivious, looking up past the high, stone palisade wall. I could hear distant chirps, whistles and dragon calls coming from the dragon enclosure. In the distance, I could even see a few dark shapes, zooming across the underside of the clouds scattered overhead. Dragons in flight practice, some with riders and some without. I thought I saw a flash of red, but I turned back to Sebastian.

He's not paying attention! I stamped my foot, making him startle and jump. He turned back to me, guilty look on his face. "Uh, sorry. I got distracted."

"I'll just have to hope you don't get distracted when we're out on patrol," I snapped. He lowered his face, and I instantly felt mean. Sebastian picked up the staff and gestured that I should try again. I nodded. "Okay, now remember you are trying to connect with the staff, to parry it away." I emphasized the movements as I spoke, showing him how he could twist his wrists to turn his own staff and catch my own blows.

And then I swung.

Sebastian pulled up his hand just in time, flinching as he did so and half-closing his eyes. I stopped my staff just short of wrapping him on the knuckles, knowing from past experience how much that would hurt. If I connected, he would just drop his staff.

I swung from a different angle, a really easy, two-handed swipe. All he had to do was push out with two hands on his own staff to catch mine. He flinched again, raising his arms too late, tangling his staff into mine. My staff thudded into his shoulder and he slipped, one hand grabbing my own arm and bringing me tumbling down with him in a desperate attempt to steady himself.

I hit the ground and air whooshed out of my lungs. The sand hurt. I spat out a bite of dirt and rolled off him. "By the First

Dragon!" I stood, my face hot and bruises sore. I heard the laughter from the other trainees. Everyone had seen that.

Everyone knows I've got no chance of surviving in the saddle with this stupid peasant.

"Sorry…sorry, Thea. I tripped." Sebastian got to his feet, wincing and brushing at himself. We all wore the uniforms of trainees now—a leather jerkin over a cotton tunic, and thick cotton trousers and boots. The cotton clothes were as fine as any I had at home, and the leather jerkins were in the colours to match our dragons. Somehow, Sebastian still managed to look dirty and unkempt in his academy clothes, his hair was still a wild mess, and while he didn't stink, he just didn't look like he belonged. But if he went, I did too. That meant I had to make this work somehow.

I glared at him, but muttered in a tight voice, "It's fine. Fine!" From the look in his eyes, I could tell he didn't believe it was. He's going to let me down. All the hard work I was putting in was going to be wasted. I felt miserable. I just wanted to make Father proud of me. I wanted to prove to them all that I was worthy of being here, as I was from the House of Flamma. And Sebastian could mean I ended up getting kicked out.

He looked at me like a kicked puppy, but before I could try to explain things to him again, one of the dragon horns blew. Weapons practice was over for the afternoon. We only had an hour to clean up before the evening meal. We were on free time.

"Okay. We'll get it tomorrow," I said, dismissing him with a shaken nod. I turned to the weapons sheds to take back our staves. I heard Sebastian say something, but I was already walking away. I felt bad for ignoring him, but he needed something to make him start paying attention. I didn't know if it made him feel any better, but I also ignored Shakasta who tried to start a conversation with me about how hopeless my partner was. I didn't want to hear that.

With a sigh and a groan, I put the quarterstaffs back in their stacks by the door of the shed. I seized a short bow and a quiver of practice arrows. I had time before the meal and archery had always helped to clear my head. The concentration of it calmed my nerves.

The academy was really mostly practice yard, when all was considered. The stone walls had six towers that formed a circle around the old keep. The keep was made up of a bunch of buildings all made of stone with a kitchen, a kitchen garden, the great hall where we met, the room where we dined and had lessons with its long tables, the rooms where we slept with two or five to a room, the store rooms, and then a lot of open space between the tower walls and the keep. I'd learned that in times of emergency, a dragon carrying a wounded rider could land right inside the academy, between the walls and the keep. The open space left a lot of room for weapons drills, and the archery range stood at one end of that space, round targets fixed to straw dummies shaped like enemy warriors.

Taking up a position in front of the targets, I put my arrows onto the ground where I could reach them. I breathed deep, centering myself, allowing my mind to become focused on one point. Fitting an arrow to the bow-string, I aimed and took a shot. I liked to shoot quickly, a skill my brothers had told me was worth learning for us in a dragon saddle. Don't wait to find the target—find the target with your hands and your eyes as you draw. I moved, my hand tracking up, my eyes finding the painted red center heart of the target, allowing my aim to settle for barely a half a second, then firing.

The arrow shot out, hitting the target just a finger away from the red dot. Curse it! I rolled my shoulders to relax my muscles, let breath pool in my chest and let my head empty.

Quick movements. Arrow to bow-string, nock and draw.

Find the target. There!

Draw a little further. Breathe out—release.

This time the arrow kissed the edge of the large, red dot.

"Good, but I've seen a better aim from your brother." I turned to the voice behind me and saw a tall, young man striding toward me.

I recognized him at once. "Prince Justin." I gave him a low

bow.

Justin was, I had to admit, pretty handsome. He had jaw-length, blond hair cut sharply, high cheekbones and deep blue eyes that seemed always to hold a laugh. I stared at him wondering why he looked better today than he ever had as a boy. Was it because now he wore a Dragon Rider's armor? In the late afternoon sun, the metal gleamed silver over his broad chest, and the leather on his arms and legs was as supple and fine as any I'd ever seen. As a boy in fine silks and ruffles, he'd never been this good-looking.

"Lady Agathea." Prince Justin bowed. He gave me a crooked smile, and the heat rushed up my neck and into my face. He leaned close and said, "I still remember when you used to put rock lizards down the back of my shirt."

I winced. "Ah. You remember that." House Flamma had always been close allies with the rulers of Torvald. As children, we had all been at the same spring and summer festivities. My mother had always told me to behave as fit the House Flamma, but I had not always listened. The young Prince Justin and I met as only toddlers— he had been a lot pudgier than he was now and I hadn't liked how he'd stolen my apple tarts. I hadn't seen him in years, however. When Ryan's green dragon had decided to match Ryan with Prince Justin, Father had been delighted, but it had taken both Ryan and the prince into the duties of Dragon Riders. Ryan was always telling me about some new tale of adventure and about the bravery of Prince Justin, but the prince was often on patrol, and so we had rarely met since early childhood.

He gave a laugh. "Yes, I do remember, and I remember that it was my fault for being unkind to you." He pointed at the archery range. "I should have known you'd be a good archer. Even back then you always wanted to run after the boys and copy them."

"Growing up with two older brothers, my lord, leaves a girl feeling she must be as good as them."

"Thankfully, you have not grown up to have their rough looks as well." My face heated even hotter, so did the rest of my body. He took my bow from my hands. "Let's see how good a match you are for me."

He seized up an arrow. He drew the bow back, and I could see the strength of his arms and chest flexing. He breathed in—so did I—and released the arrow.

The arrow hit with a hard sound and quivered just a few fingers off center.

"Very good, my lord," I said, accepting my bow back.

"Oh, just Justin, please. I am not ready to be lord of all the realm yet." He gave a wide grin.

Mouth set, I was determined to best him. I felt as if he was amused by me, and not thinking I could ever pose a serious threat to anyone. Breathe. Draw. Aim. My arrow hit and quivered next to his, inside the red circle, but not as close as his to the center.

"Well done!" he said, his eyes narrowing, but with his mouth still curved. I did not think he meant the words. He turned to me. "How's the training going? I saw you sparring, you know. You're good with a quarterstaff."

"Better with a sword." I walked with him to retrieve our arrows. I wondered if I could tell him the truth about my frustrations. There was no one else I could really talk to. The other trainees, such as Beris, were too cruel, too eager to make a joke of everything. My brothers were busy with the training of the young dragons, and Prince Justin was the only one apart from my brothers who knew me well, or who at least knew me from my early years.

"It's Sebastian, my partner. I'm…worried for him, quite frankly," I said in a rush.

"Worried for him?" Prince Justin frowned. He sounded as if he thought perhaps I worried for my own place, and I didn't.

I pulled out an arrow. "He's not like the others. He's strong enough…he is a blacksmith's boy, as you must know. But he doesn't know how to use that strength. He's had no training, no horsemanship, no fencing, and no skills." I let out a sigh. "He is affecting both our chances of doing well in the tests. What if we let everyone down?" This worry kept me up most nights. "What if he fails? Or worse…if he is unable to do all that a rider must to

44

get our dragon back to Mount Hammal safe after every ride."

The prince pulled out his arrow and handed it to me. "Remember, Thea, it was the dragon that chose both of you. I'm sure that the boy will pick up what he must. He's probably just a late bloomer." He smiled reassuringly at me, again with that crooked twist of his mouth that made it seem as if he knew more than he was saying. "I'll be keeping an eye on your progress. I can't wait to see another Flamma up in the skies with us. Try not to worry so about your partner. Trust that your dragon knew what it was about."

"Yes, my…Justin. I'll try."

He touched a finger to my cheek. "You do that. Now I've got to go to some ridiculous ball tonight, so I must be off. My father tells me I spend too much time with my dragon, and not enough with my other duties. But I'll tell Ryan and Reynalt you're still as wild as ever." He gave me a grin and set off across the practice ground, his long legs taking him away all too fast.

I watched him until he vanished into a doorway that led to out of the academy and along the road back into the city where the king's castle stood. It was good to see someone who had once known me, and to be friends again, after so long. But did Prince Justin really have any idea of how hard these tests were going to be for me with Sebastian in tow?

CHAPTER 6

HOW TO FIND YOUR WAY

I picked up my staff and gave the edge of the wall a few experimental jabs to try and get the hang of what Thea was telling me. Behind me, she was already rummaging about in the weapons shed, leaving me to try and figure this out.

Just raise it a bit higher…and… I jabbed the edge of the wall. The shock of impact traveled down my forearms as if the thing was alive, making me drop the staff. It felt a wiggling snake.

"Can't even win against an inanimate object," one of the other boys muttered. Stooping, I grabbed the long stick and looked up to see Beris. Next to him, Shakasta was trying to stifle his laughter. The two shook their heads and filed into the keep's kitchens.

I coughed, standing up with my cheeks burning.

"Maybe they're right. Maybe I should just give up now," I muttered to myself, inspecting the grazes on my knuckles and the bruises on my forearms. What do I know about fighting? Who'd ever heard of a peasant from the streets becoming one of the Dragon Riders of Torvald, famous throughout the realms? I'd never twirled a fighting staff before I came here. I could pound a hammer and chop with an axe, but with this staff, I seemed to

46

become nothing but thumbs and wrong moves.

I kicked the dust, scuffing the new, simple leather boots the instructors had given me. All my clothes were new, with a brown tunic and trousers, and a leather jerkin that did nothing to keep the bruises from forming. Even wearing the same clothes I still looked out of place compared to the others who all came from noble families. Somehow they managed to look right in the uniform, but mine just seemed not to fit. I threw down my staff and stared at it.

"You certainly won't get very far with that attitude."

I looked up to see a bristling moustache and the rest of Commander Hegarty. He stood in one of the archways of the stone avenue that connected the keep to the towers.

"Commander, sir, I'm sorry, I didn't see you there." I tried to bow, not knowing how far I should go.

"No need to stand on ceremony, Smith. You are here to learn how to be a warrior, and you won't learn that by throwing down your weapon," his voice sounded gruff, but I heard a touch of feeling there for me. He fixed me with a measuring, assessing eye. "Tell me Sebastian, have you seen the map room up in the observation tower yet? Maybe it will be more to your liking."

There was still an hour before the horn sounded for dinner—and I was ready to do anything to avoid having to go another round with Thea and a staff. I nodded and tried not to sound too eager. "I'd love to, sir."

"Come with me, Sebastian," he turned and started walking quickly along the stone avenue, his boots clipping on the cobbles as he did so.

The observation tower was the tallest tower at the academy. It stuck out from the side of the mountain like a finger pointing to the sky. From this grand tower, the scribes and scouts could prepare and catalogue their scrolls for the navigators. I'd often looked up at the roof—tiled with dark slate—from the small space outside the smithy many leagues below and wondered what it must be like inside.

Commander Hegarty nudged open a heavy, wooden door, revealing a set of spiraling stone steps and a winch-lift, a wooden platform built like a box with a series of weights attached to a cogwheel. I knew that was used for when the scouts had to get to the top of the tower in very short time—they could rise up on this when the weights were released, shooting up as if they had dragon wings. Thankfully, Commander Hegarty informed me now that we would be taking the more sedate, stairwell route.

The commander went up the many hundreds of steps with a spry step. I followed, my legs starting to ache and my chest was heaving. He didn't even seem out of breath. I wondered just how often he had made this journey and if he even noticed how high it was. As we walked, he talked and I looked out of the narrow windows that we passed on our way up, watching the academy open space getting ever smaller beneath. The terraced and walled city of Torvald now looked more like an ant nest, it was so small.

"Where are you from, Sebastian?" Hegarty asked. "I can see that you haven't had any training."

I stared the steps and his boots and my feet. "I'm from Monger's Lane," I said, mumbling the words.

"Near Old Bridge, am I right, and the gate where the woodworkers come into the city?"

"That's right, sir." I glanced up, amazed that a man in his position had even heard of us.

Hegarty glanced back and his mustache twitched. "You may be surprised to hear this, Sebastian, but a very long time ago, I grew up in Old Bridge myself. My father and mother were woodcutters. We used to spend all our time roaming the woods on the eastern side of Mount Hammal, looking after the forest there. I was all set to join them in their work before my dragon, Heclaxia, chose me."

I almost stumbled in my steps. "You, you were poor, sir?"

Hegarty chuckled in the way a bear might when presented with a strange joke or an easy meal. "Do I not look it now?" He looked down at his Dragon Riders' armor, and then at his breeches and sturdy boots. "I guess these simple things must look like finery. I remember a time when even a pair of shoes was a luxury."

I hung my head. It seemed a comfort to know the commander knew something of my troubles, but I still felt out of place. "I'm sorry, sir, I didn't mean any disrespect."

"And none taken, Sebastian. But you need to have a little more faith in yourself. Your dragon saw something in you. That's good enough for anyone, or it should be. I heard tell you are a blacksmith's son, is that right?" Hegarty carried on up the stairs.

"Yes, sir. Worked night and day in the Monger's Lane smithy for my da…" I ran out of words as I remembered just what that work meant. Hours of shifting full barrows of ore, ingots, coal and wood. Not much actual blacksmithing for me, just hard labor. "But, uh, I didn't get to do a lot. My da said I was too clumsy."

Not that it stopped him from drinking, shouting and pouring the lead wrong and spilling the ore, I thought with a flash of anger, my fists balling at my sides.

"Hmm."

I looked up to see the commander once again looking at me with those sharp eyes of his that seemed to see a lot. He didn't push me for an answer, but kept his brisk walk up the steps. After a moment, he said, "It can be difficult, being poor. A lot of challenges that some others don't face."

I nodded. I knew he would say no more on the subject, and neither would I. It seemed like an unspoken understanding had passed between us. We shared a history of coming up from nothing, and I felt like he was telling me the past was gone now. I felt odd about it, and let out a breath.

"Hera- Hecla..?" I tried to say, forming my mouth around the odd word he had said.

"He-clax-ia," Hegarty said, drawing out the word, his voice losing its hard edge for a moment so it seemed soft and gentle as a breeze. "That was my dragon. Oh, she was a beauty. A red like yours."

"A red? You rode a red?" My jaw dropped before the thought hit me. Was. "Oh, I'm sorry, sir. She was your dragon?"

"Yes." Hegarty's step faltered, slowed and stopped. "Poor Heclaxia. She is no longer my dragon, but lives in the enclosure with the others. My navigator—he caught an arrow in the neck right in front of me as we were chasing some pirates along the Coast of Kidjia'an. It was a miracle we even made it back to Torvald at all, but Heclaxia knew what she was doing." He looked at me with a deep sadness in his eyes. "Dragons only choose once, boy, and when their riders are dead and gone, they return to the enclosure to become brood mothers or stud fathers. Heclaxia has a big cave up on the eastern side of Mount Hammal. I still hike out to see her when I can, but she's more intent on snapping at the younger dragons and telling them how to raise their eggs."

I was confused. "I—I'm sorry sir, but you talk about…about your red as if…" I stammered, thinking I was putting my boots into something that could be raw as a burn from the forge.

"As if she can talk? As if they have names?" Hegarty started up the worn steps again and his gruff chuckle came back into his voice. "That's because they can boy, although I've never heard them. The dragon tells the navigator its name. Some navigators can even talk to them." Hegarty shook his head as if it was all a mystery to him. "I was just a protector, but my navigator told me our red's name, and after he was gone I was all she had left. That's why it's important that you have both navigator and protector on board a dragon. They keep each other safe." He stopped as we reached a landing. "And here we are. In you go, Sebastian. Tell Merik I sent you and you'll be free to use this place whenever you have free time."

He pushed open the door and ushered me inside before turning and without even pausing to catch his breath, he jogged back down the stairs. I could hear his boots clacking and growing fainter as I thought over what he had just shared.

Dragons have names. Dragons can talk. It doesn't matter where you come from, it's the dragon that chose you.

"Hey," said a light voice. I looked up, startled to see another youth in the map room. He was older than me by a good few years, maybe even into his twenties. He looked thin and elongated, kind of like a spider or a stalk. His skin was dark and his hair black as coal before it goes into the forge. He wore dull, dusty robes, not armor. On his nose there perched a small pair of optics, making his brown eyes look large as he peered at me.

"Uh…Merik?" I said uncertainly. "My name is Seb, Sebastian."

"And Merik, Merik is me." He smiled, his teeth a brilliant white against his dark skin. "I guess you could say I'm the permanent fixture about here. They all thought I had the gift for navigating—even my dragon, but with these." He tapped his optics. "It made it unlikely to ride where I could not see." He let out a sigh.

I wanted to ask where his dragon was, but I didn't dare. I didn't want to hear his dragon had gotten sick.

Looking up at me suddenly, he grinned. "Luckily, however, I have full access to the telescopes. I can see all I want. I just can't fly…not yet."

"Telly-scup?" I said, wondering if we spoke the same tongue.

The round room around me was tall with high, vaulted windows on all sides, some at ground level, others halfway up the walls, each covered with thick wooden shutters. Only a few were opened and in front of them stood strange tripods with long barrels like very thin cannons atop them. But they weren't the most overwhelming thing about this room.

Papers and tablets seemed to be everywhere. Racks and shelves of scrolls stretched from the floor to the ceiling and lay on tables. Ladders on little caster wheels stood between the shelves, and in the center of the room a large oak, work-scarred table stood. I walked over to stare at a map, so beautiful it took my breath. My ma had taught me to read, insisted on it, saying no child of hers would be dumb to knowing accounts and how to read a bill of sale. It was good business sense, she'd told my da, and he'd never been able to say no to her. But that was before the sickness swept through our lane and took her one hard winter. I'd kept up with the reading of the few papers she'd left behind, but I'd never seen the likes of this.

"Wow." I traced a finger over the shapes and designs on the map—and the words. Some of the lines looked like a child's drawing of castles and triangle-mountains. On another map I glimpsed coloured blobs with lines radiating across them. The colours were wrong, of course, but something about one of the shapes—a large, almost tear-drop shape with smaller semicircles along one side—stood in my memory.

"Oh, that's Mount Hammal. And there's the terraces of Torvald." I pointed out the different semi-circles and the circle of the crater of the dragon enclosure next to us. It looked like the

54

shape I had seen of the mountain and the city underneath me as I had walked up the steps of the tower.

"Not many people get that first time around," Merik said approvingly. "But yes, you're right. You see, these are aerial maps."

"What's—air-a-real?" I asked.

"Maps of the air, we've got some of those as well. They're called weather maps, but these are maps of what the ground looks like from the air when you're flying up above it and looking down from your dragon. Aerial."

"Oh, I see."

He gave a nod. "The colours are different so you can identify different ground features easily. White for the highest peaks of the landscape, then down the scale, so yellow next high, reds are like rolling hills, greens for valleys… You get the picture."

I did, and what was more, I knew I could read these very easily.

Merik walked me through a couple of the basic maps of the city and our nearest territories within the realm. He explained there were always at least three, sometimes four, maps of an area that a good navigator had to keep in mind at all times. The pictorial maps showed what the area looked like from the ground, with pictures of castles and cities and mountains like cracked teeth. The aerial maps detailed how the world looked from above. Current or weather maps would show the navigator what the prevailing winds and the weather was like in a region. Finally, action maps gave the boundaries between realms, marking out towns, cities and recent battles or troops moving on the ground.

"Action maps are where it gets really exciting," he grinned. "We get reports from our scouts and riders all the time, and we have to update the maps and let the navigators know just what is happening. You see there?" he pointed up to one of the odd, tripod-shaped telly-scups.

"When it's all go, I and the others look through those. They're like really good optics that make the far away seem closer. We use a system of flags and hand signals to then tell the riders and others what's happening."

"Oh. I see," I didn't, but it was fun hearing him talk with such excitement in his voice. For once, the learning felt right. I had no doubt I would pick up all the meanings and master them faster than the others. A flare of real hope warmed my chest and belly. I might be really good at something dragon-related after all.

"You see this?" he picked up a small, red flag on a stick and waved it in a looping pattern in front of him. "This is a general warning to say something's up, trouble, look out."

"And then there's this," he held the stick-flag straight up. "That means important information, hang on, I've got something for you to know." Merik laughed and I knew he must be seeing the frown on my face as I tried to keep all this in mind. "There's hundreds of them, all different coloured flags."

"But what if the riders are too far to see the observation tower?" I asked.

Merik grinned. "Well, that's the good news. You'll all have your own telescopes and if you are even too far away with them, then I wave to one of our scouts. Or other towers, and they repeat the gesture you see, all the way down the line."

"Wow, okay."

"But really, that's just a mechanism for controlling dragon traffic around Torvald and the nearby realms. When you're out there in the deep wilds you're on your own," Merik said and gave a firm nod.

"No, I won't be." I met his stare. "I will have Thea and our dragon." I felt proud of my fellow rider. She was strong and brave and even though she looked down at me at times and whacked me with a staff, I knew she would always do her best.

"Ah. Agathea Flamma?" Merik nodded. "You've got a tall order there, haven't you?"

"What do you mean?" I felt strangely defensive about my other rider, even though I could guess what he was about to say.

"Well, she's a Flamma, isn't she? They're like, the best

Dragon Riders ever. Her brother is navigator to Prince Justin, by the First Dragon's breath! And Reynalt Flamma, he captain's his own squadron for the throne. Not many of his age could say they have such an honor."

"Yeah," I said my voice dropping low. "Thanks for reminding me, as if I don't have enough to worry about with all the stuff in my head and the training and the like!"

"What? You're a Dragon Rider, by all that's above us and below, and that's not enough for you?" Merik looked at me like I was crazy. "What have you got to worry about?"

"I'm just... so bad at fighting. And I'm always near the back when we run." I slapped my legs. "I wasn't made for fast. Every time I look at Thea, she's looking back at me like I'm a big failure, and I just know that I'm letting her down!"

"She's stuck-up, just like all the other Flammas," Merik grumbled.

"No, she's not. She's hard-working. She wants to do the best she can." I heard my voice come out a little angry, so I bit off the words. It just didn't seem fair that this...this Merik could have such quick opinions of my partner. Well, maybe she is a little stuck-up, but she did come right to my side that first day. I knew she was trying to help me, even if she did so on the end of a stick that kept slapping me.

"No, okay, I'm sorry." Merik put a hand on my shoulder and shook hard. "It's a good sign you're jumping to the defense of your other rider. Just remember, you've got to trust in your own instincts as well. And I think you're good at this." He stabbed a long, stick-like finger down on the table surface between us. I smiled. He was right—I could be good at this. Now I just had to prove it to everyone.

CHAPTER 7

IMPROVEMENTS

I tried not to think about Sebastian too much. My days fit into a pattern of up early every morning, go for a quick run, get washed, have breakfast and hit the practice yards. I wanted to stay focused, but that was harder than it sounded. As the days slipped past, he was getting better, but not as quickly as he should. Compared with Beris and Jensen and others, he was so far behind in the fighting skills that I feared he would never catch up.

Added to this, he had started to go off on his own. I followed him one day and saw him head up into the observation tower. I knew some skinny kid—one of the scribes or scholars or someone called Merik or Erik or something—hung out there in the map room. And Sebastian started to talk about how this map sign meant one thing and that wave of a flag meant whatever else. I had to press my lips tight to tell him that wasn't what he needed to learn.

To me, trying to keep Sebastian's thoughts on learning what he should be learning was like trying to keep a crowd of bees in one place. All of the facts he kept telling me overflowed. As soon as I remembered a couple of things, I would lose the third! It made me happy to see he was finally getting some of his training, but I just wished he was better at the fighting and physical stuff.

He was a guy, after all. Everyone, including me, expected he would become the protector. To be honest, if the commander announced tomorrow that Sebastian was going to be my protector, I'd be tempted to turn around and punch Sebastian for failing me and his dragon.

I heard a grunt of pain from across the courtyard and sighed. I was trading practice blows with others, and doing fairly well, I had to admit. That yelp, however, had unmistakably come from Sebastian as he sparred with Jensen.

I was fighting Wil who was not that great with a staff. He had a few more tricks than some I had sparred against in the noble schools, but he was no real match for me. I had to focus on trying not to defeat him too easily, giving myself the challenge of seeing how many of his strikes I could parry or dodge without returning them. The game I was playing gave me a chance to slide a quick glance over to where Sebastian was being helped up by Jensen, and they were both smirking at each other.

Just like Sebastian, making friends with the person he's supposed to be attacking. A smile curled my lips.

I parried another blow that flew toward my ear, turning on my heel to present a different stance to my opponent. Sebastian was a nice guy, but nice was not going to make him into a Dragon Rider.

My staff rattled in my hands as I parried another blow.

He was easy to like, was Sebastian. He had an open manner and a quick laugh, and treated everyone the same. He was already getting an extra bowl of meat broth or a fresh bread roll from the kitchens. I knew the cooks thought he looked half-starved, and Sebastian shared his extras with me. It was easy to be nice to him.

I ducked a wild swing from Wil, noting he was starting to pant and sweat from the exertion and putting out too much effort. If he wasn't careful, Wil would spend all of his energy trying to attack and have none left for any defense when I moved against him.

That thought left me frowning and thinking about Sebastian— Seb, he kept saying I should call him. He put out so much effort to try to be my friend, but I blocked every effort as if it was a blow meant to hit. The problem was that I was too aware of how well my brothers had done in the academy. The Flammas were all supposed to be not just excellent Dragon Riders but the best of the best. I was putting all the pressure that I felt onto Seb, too. I thought he should be the best, too.

Shame for how I'd been acting made me bite my lip. This was not how a Flamma or a Dragon Rider should act.

A hard jolt hit me on the side of my thigh, and I realized I had allowed my worries to distract me from the fight.

"Ha!" Wil said, stepping back and smiling. "A point to me." He raised his staff to wave it at Beris and Shakasta.

Oh, no you don't! I rapped my staff on the ground, drawing his attention back to the fact that I was still standing, armed and dangerous. I even gave him time to assume a defensive posture before I easily parried his first jab, leaned in and neatly hooked him behind the knee and levered him to the ground.

He hit the sand like a sack of potatoes.

I prodded him not too gently on the chest. "Point to me, and you're incapacitated," I said, not really feeling any joy in the win. I should have kept my mind on the fight instead of wondering about Sebastian…Seb.

Wil made a disgruntled noise. Reaching down, I helped him up. "Why do I get the impression you could have done that sooner?" he muttered. We walked back to the benches for cold water and a towel for Wil's sweating face.

I was halfway through telling him what I could have done when I heard the *thock-thock* of wooden staves against each other. Turning, I saw Sebastian and Jensen were still fighting. I turned to watch the two of them.

After me, Jensen was probably the best fighter. Either Jensen or Beris maybe. It was more than clear that Sebastian hadn't had any real training. He was still slow to react, still moved cautiously when he should be fast. He was too quick to drop his staff instead of hanging onto it, and he was too easily distracted by other things.

Jensen was definitely winning, but I saw Sebastian pull off the across the body defensive movement I had taught him. A little surge of pride lifted inside me. *Seb is getting better.* I watched as Jensen grinned fiercely, prodding and swiping. Sebastian parried, and parried again.

A small hope started to flare like a candle. *Go on, Seb!* I silently urged him. He made a few tentative stabs back at Jensen. His attacks were faint though and ill-timed. He didn't give everything to them. Jensen waited for the next sweep of Sebastian's staff. He batted Sebastian's staff aside with a powerful blow and delivered a hard prod to Sebastian's stomach. Seb dropped his staff and sat down hard.

Coughing, Sebastian clutched his middle. That flicker of hope turned into a cold grip of worry. *Is he hurt?* I started toward them, but heard Seb give a wheezing laugh. Jensen offered him a hand to pull him up. They were both slapping each other on the back.

"By the First Dragon, I thought you were going to disembowel me!" Sebastian said with a wry smile.

"Not with a stave, you idiot." Jensen laughed. "You lasted longer than the others."

"Thanks." Sebastian's smile faded as I walk up to him. "Thea, did you see that? Last to die...almost." He smiled at me.

I found myself smiling at his enthusiasm despite the fact that I knew I should yell at him for missing that last parry he should have made. I shook my head and turned, so he wouldn't see that I was secretly pleased for him. "Come on. You might be dead, but you smell like you need a wash."

"Oh, thanks," Seb protested.

Walking ahead of him, I thought Prince Justin might have been right. The dragon had chosen Sebastian—Seb. The dragon had seen not just strength in him, but also something more. I was starting to see it too. He was getting better—there might just be a chance than we could do well at the trials that were almost on us.

CHAPTER 8

THE TRIALS

The morning of the trials I woke early from bad dreams, certain I was going to fail Thea. Fail everyone, my dragon included. My stomach hurt as if I had eaten too many green apples and my head felt like it was going to pop off of my shoulders at any moment.

I'm going to fail. I'm going to fail. Everyone is going to hate me—especially Thea.

Despite the fact that I had been training as hard as I could, even doing extra running practice every morning before breakfast, and then running up the stairs of the observation tower to eat lunch with Merik and practice map reading, I still felt I was the worst trainee in the academy.

Every single day had turned into a long slog, worse than anything I'd had to go through with the smithy. I did hours of running, climbing and painful weapons practice. And trying to teach Thea all the basic flag movements and their meanings was even worse. She no sooner figured out one thing than she forgot the previous one. But every scrap of praise or encouragement she gave me felt like gold dust in my hand. But I knew it was not enough. I could tell from how Thea watched me, shaking her head at times and disappointment in her eyes, she thought I would fail at everything related to fighting skills. I thought it, too.

The teachers kept saying it wasn't about winning or failing, it was about finding out what we could do. I knew differently. If I did the worst, if I came last at everything, the other Dragon Riders would never respect me. Worse still, Thea would never respect me. She would never trust me, and how could we ever be riders together if that was the case?

I have to do well. I just have to!

The best of us, or so I heard as the trainees talked at meals, was either Thea or Beris. Beris was stronger, but Thea was faster. They were both gifted with stamina and it showed that they had been preparing for this their whole lives. When it came to the sword, they both knew moves I could never copy. Beris was a little better at the staff, but Thea was better with the bow and arrow. The rest of us could only try to be as good.

If it was working out how much iron ore you needed for a plough, I could win that test. For the rest, I was sure I would fail my dragon and be sent home in shame. Shaking my head, I slipped from my bunk and headed for the kitchens to get breakfast. But I knew the knots tying up my insides would leave me unable to eat so much as a spoonful of porridge.

The others who shared a room with me were already up and gone. I dressed quickly and headed to the hall where we dined. "I hope you are ready to buy me a celebratory flagon of ale down at the Troll's Head later." Beris skewered several pieces of bacon from the serving tray and heaped his plate. He did this every morning, and I hated how he announced to everyone just how great he was and terrible they all were. It was one thing to believe in yourself, but Beris loved to rub it in how great he was. As if no one else mattered.

"I'm ready to pour a flagon of ale over your head," Shakasta said and tucked into his own meat sandwich.

"Why waste it?" Syl saw me slink and nodded my direction. "Unless, of course, someone could do with washing their hair."

Snickers followed me to the tables. I tried to ignore them. I wasn't dirty, I bathed more often now than anyone else apart from Thea. Years of working in a forge and foundry had taught me to clean when you could. But the fact that I'd grown up in the poorest part of town had turned into a running joke. Today, I didn't care what they said. What I did would be all that mattered. By tonight, everything would be different, one way or another.

"Easy, Syl." Thea had come into the room, her hair wet and dark from water. I knew she had already been up, swimming in the crystal clear lake on the other side of the ridge, training hard to make sure she performed well today.

I'm not the only one nervous about today's trials, then.

"So, the trials," Thea announced to everyone. "Anyone know

what we've got?"

Beris looked up, eager as always to show how much he knew. "I hear there are tests all the way through the morning with experienced Dragon Riders assessing us. We'll be fighting—we have to show we are fit enough to stay on a dragon." He flexed his arms. "And it'll be lots of me winning every test!"

The first horn of the morning rang, signaling we had to finish our meal and get ourselves washed and ready. The second horn would signal the beginning of the tests. My stomach knotted. I stared at the platter of meat, bread and fruit on the table, and I wanted to run from the room.

From next to me, her voice low, Thea said, "Eat. You'll need it."

"Thanks." She probably just doesn't want me to faint in front of everyone. I picked up a slab of bread. I started to turn, but a hand fell on my arm.

"And Seb?" Thea said. She stared up at me, her eyes huge and blue.

"Yeah?" I dreaded what was going to come next. She would tell me to be faster, to be stronger, and not ruin this for her.

"Good luck. You've improved a lot." She gave a faint smile. I pushed out my chest. She'd never talked so well toward me. I knew she was probably just trying to boost my confidence, but I

69

didn't mind. It was working. For her I would try to do the impossible—I would try not to fail.

Following Thea, I ate my bread and headed for the training grounds. We would assemble there. The bread tasted dry in my mouth, and I only managed to get two bites down. I fed the rest to one of the kitchen cats, who took it and hunched over it as if I had fed it a treat. The second Dragon Horn reverberated through the chill morning air of the academy.

We had already assembled in a long line along one side, and the sun was still below the palisade walls where it would creep up over the next few hours to turn this cool, shady area into a furnace. It would shimmer with dust and sand, reflecting the bowl of the sky above. I could hear the chirrups and caws of the dragons over the ridge in their enclosure, greeting the sun and waking to the sound of the horns. They, too, were going to be readied for the next stage of training, fitted with harnesses and saddles. At the end of the tests, trainees—scrubs—would be presented again to the dragons, and we would see if we could start training as a team and as cadets.

I was surprised to see Merik standing with the rest of the trainees, his thin body taller than most and leaner. Walking over to him, I gave him a smile. "Merik, I thought that you couldn't, um, you know." I waved at his face and his optics.

"Fly?" he grinned and nodded at the instructors who had

assembled on the platform above us. "The commander said he would give me another try. See if I can make it this time, and then I just need a dragon to pick me." He sighed. "The dragon who chose me that first time—the sickness took her."

I shivered. Dragon sickness wasn't common, but when it hit, I knew it almost always killed. No wonder the academy had felt bad for Merik and let him stay on—any rider would mourn the loss of a dragon, particularly a young one who never had a chance to prove itself. I slapped Merik's shoulder. "Good luck!" I said to him. The training ground had fallen silent and a wave of tension seemed to sweep over all of us.

"You too," he whispered back.

Commander Hegarty's voice rang out over the clear morning air. He was standing atop one of the landing platforms, calling down to us. "Trainees of Dragon Academy! Students of Torvald! Today is a great day in your training! Today you shall be tested and we will assign you your roles. Either you will become protector or navigator. We will also find out what sort of person you are, and what sort of rider you will become. Or you are someone who might die all too soon in service to the king."

I gulped. I knew I could end up being sent home. Or maybe even end up with a lifetime of scaring cattle rustlers around Mount Hammal, or perhaps I would get to explore the distant wilds, even going as far as the Great Western Archipelago, or flying further than any Dragon Rider had ever gone before. I swallowed the dryness in my mouth.

"But today is about more than that! Today is about you. It is about you showing your fellow rider what you can do. It is about you reaching beyond your limits and proving you are worthy to sit in a dragon's saddle. It is about you becoming ready to ride your dragons!"

All of us opened our mouth in a throaty roar of celebration. We wanted to prove ourselves. We wanted to be the best.

"With me here there are some of the best Dragon Riders, past and present, in the king's service. They will help me make my decisions. Good luck, trainees! May the winds guide you forward and the sun warm your backs!" he raised a hand in a salute, signaling for the trials to begin.

The Dragon Horn blew for a third time. Heart pounding, I walked with the others to where we were directed. Two Dragon Riders stood before the main gates. They motioned us into a line and said we would start with a simple race to get us warmed up. I almost groaned. I hated running. Back home, I'd never had to run more than up the street to fetch wood, and now I had to run and run and run. The gates were cranked open, and we were told to complete a circuit out to the ridge and back again.

With the beat of a drum, we shot off across the arena. I was grateful now for my boots. They bit into the gravel and dust and stone and I told myself I would at least keep up with the others.

Within seconds, we had run past the thick stone walls. The early morning air of Mount Hammal stung my face and my lungs. The terraces of the city spread out below and the winding, stone lane that ran from the academy down to the city below stood out in contrast within the grey morning shadows. We were taking a different path than we usually did. The path had been marked with flags. The lane narrowed to a goat track with barely room for two abreast. We had to skitter between boulders and mountain streams, running up to the ridge.

My legs were still cold and from how others staggered I knew they felt the same. Everyone bunched in a large gaggle at first. Shakasta was the first to break away, using his longer, limber frame to leap past the rocks as gracefully as any mountain sheep. I struggled along, feet pounding hard on the ground, trying to remember how to breathe, and looking for openings that I could exploit.

My calves and thighs burned as we ran, but I was having no trouble keeping pace with the others. I'd always had to move, push, haul, but I hated running.

"Pace yourself," said a voice beside me. I glanced back to see Thea running just behind me. After a moment, I realized she wasn't pushing herself and I caught her meaning. Save something for the return.

I slowed down and matched her speed. We reached the long, thin ridge with the two of us near the back of the pack. Touching the capstone rock, I let myself go as I sped back downhill. The energy I had saved made it easy for me to pass a half dozen others. I was closing on the ones in front. Surprisingly, I saw Merik in the lead, his long and lean frame—and doubtless all that running up and down the observation tower—giving him an advantage in this trial.

I thought I might be top five, but then Thea passed by my side like a flash. She juggled with Beris for a second at third position and then she moved ahead of him. Beris was sweating hard.

We were almost down to the palisade again and heading in for a sprinting finish.

Beris looked back, saw me gaining on him. He frowned. Just as I was nearing him, he lashed out with an elbow, catching me in the ribs and sending me tumbling. My shin caught a boulder on the side of the track and I went down with pain lacing up my leg. With a cry, I pushed myself up, forcing myself to run to catch up. Already the front runners were crossing back through the main gate. I rejoined the race in the middle of the other runners.

The Dragon Horn sounded and I heaved to a panting stop. Dragon Riders came forward with water buckets for us. Looking down, I saw a nasty graze that covered about half the length of my lower leg. It stung like blazes. I scowled at Beris, but he wouldn't look at me.

Merik had come in first, then Jensen. Thea had beaten Beris at least, and I was happy for Merik and Thea.

I was angry now—at myself for letting Beris cheat me out of doing better and at myself for not ducking his blow. I would not let that happen again. I would stay away from him.

The next challenge started at once, and I had barely gained my breath back. It was another physical challenge. We were each issued a quarter staff and told to line up. We would be fighting in duels and would go on with the duels until one clear winner had fought to the defeat of everyone else.

I gulped. Staff fighting wasn't my best skill, even with the extra practice I had put in. My leg was also beginning to throb. Do it for your dragon, and your family! I pulled in a deep breath and tried to ready myself. The staff ends were wrapped in leather strips, cushioning them a little but still, I knew this was going to hurt.

Our first set of challenges pitted me against a boy named Tenzer. He was younger than me and from a minor noble family. We were about the same size, yet he used his staff much quicker than I. Next to us, I could hear the grunts and cracks of wood on wood as all other trainees fought. I tried to block that out. Thea was always telling me I was too easily distracted—I had to pay attention to my own duel.

Tenzer's staff whirled around. I managed to pull mine across my body, knocking his to one side. No sooner had I done that than another blow came overhead at me. I parried it again. Maybe I was starting to get the hang of this. I managed to block and parry each blow, but I found it hard to attack. I knew Tenzer. He had never been mean to me, so I didn't feel any real drive to attack and it showed in my moves. His next blow snaked forward and caught me on the knees, making me step backward.

"Point to Trainee Tenzer!" the Dragon Rider watching our duel called.

I can't let him win!

This time when Tenzer stepped forward, I let him think I was just going to parry. Instead, I moved forward with the butt of my staff, slipping it behind his heel and pulling upwards. Thea had shown me this move. Tenzer wasn't expecting it and went flying onto the dirt on his back, an instant loss.

"Win to Sebastian!" Our Dragon Rider clapped me on the shoulder. I reached down a hand to help Tenzer up. He grinned at me and didn't seem to be worried that he had lost.

I had defeated one person, as had Beris, Thea, Syl, Jensen and Wil. Merik hadn't. He'd been unfortunately teamed against Jensen, who had soundly beaten Merik. Things were looking up for me, I hoped. The next round was called. I was pitted against Beris, Thea against Syl, and Jensen against Wil.

The sun was rising higher in the sky, warming the late morning. The training area had started to heat up. I was sweating as I stepped into the marked chalk circle for my next duel. I could feel the eyes of the commander and the other Dragon Riders on me. They walked around us, passing quiet comments, and I could hear them talk about each trainee's form and technique.

There was a clap and we started. I found myself looking at a ferociously grinning Beris. He baited me by darting the butt of his staff forward, pushing at me, trying to distract me I knew.

"What are you gonna do, poor boy?" Beris hissed under his breath. "Knock me out with your stink?"

I lashed out. He caught my blow, easily turning it aside and struck back. I only just managed to get out of the way in time. I turned to see Beris advancing again, a grin on his face.

"Here! Take that!" he was saying, confident about his perfect technique. It was all I could do to block first one blow, then another, before the next blow rattled my staff. I had no time for anything but defensive moves, and barely those.

A painful slap of the staff across my bleeding shin caused me to fall to the ground. I rolled and bounced back to my feet, stick still in hand before the watching Dragon Rider could call a win for Beris. I hopped up and down on one foot for a second, panting before gingerly putting my foot down again.

He'd hit my wound on purpose, I knew. He gave a narrow-eyed look that said as much.

Beris shrugged. "What you gonna do about it?" He laughed, and I charged.

It wasn't a graceful attack, more of an outright assault, but he wasn't expecting it. I was hot-faced angry and tired of always being quiet and backing down from him. Maybe that came from being raised to think all nobles were better than me, but I was done with that.

I wasn't going to let him win.

I swung my staff and pivoted it in the palm of my hand. He parried and blocked me each time, but I was driving him further and further back. It was easy for him to block my blows, but that was my intention. I was setting him up, and he was arrogant enough to think I had no strategy working.

"Beris out. Win to Sebastian!" The Dragon Rider called and clapped his hands.

"What?" Beris suddenly stopped. He stared at the Dragon Rider, his face red and his mouth hanging open.

The Dragon Rider pointed down at our feet to where I had successfully forced Beris out of the chalk circle. Beris had been so confident he was better than me that he had forgotten the rules of the duel.

"That's not fair," Beris said. "He never even scored a hit on me!"

"Stop whining, Beris, you got to the second stage, which is better than most." The Dragon Rider nodded to me. I had time enough to watch Thea win her bout against Syl, and Jensen won his against Wil.

Beris was scowling at me as he stalked away. The chalk was redrawn. There were three contenders left, meaning two fights. I waited for the judges to call out names, and heard with dismay that I would be dueling against Thea. Jensen would fight whoever won.

"Sorry," I said to Thea and stepped into the ring.

"Don't be. You're going to lose." She gave me a tiny smile. I had to smile back. That attitude let me know she would be okay if I won or lost. I could relax and just do my best.

With a clap from the watching Dragon Rider, we started. Thea performed like I had never seen before. She didn't bother to hold the quarterstaff across her body like the rest of us, instead she twirled it over her head like a windmill before bringing it down as she spun her body across the circle with a graceful leap.

I dodged the first blow only to realize the move had been a trick. She switched her grip lightning fast and sent a rapid blister of blows against me, landing a hit on my hip and then on my head.

I tried to raise my staff to defend myself, but she had done something strange with her own staff which forced mine out of my hands. Another blow from nowhere to the back of my knees sent me to the floor, weaponless.

"Yield?" she said, standing over me.

I moaned an answer and bowed over in pain.

"Sebastian out. Win to Thea!" The Dragon Rider clapped to end the match. Others had gathered to watch and were clapping for Thea. I was glad for her. She had worked really hard to get this good.

I limped out of the fighting circle, and the last fight between Jensen and Thea was being prepared. Sipping a cup of mountain water, I again watched the way Thea spun her stick faster than a dragon's tail could spin, diving the staff around her body as if it was part of her. It was almost like she was dancing, lashing out with blows faster than anything we could manage.

But Jensen was good. He didn't twirl his staff, but used it almost like a spear, one end stabbing, sweeping and making a wide space around him. It was hard for Thea to get past his attacks. He scored the first hit on her shins.

After that, Thea just moved quicker. When Jensen lunged forward in a strike that should have knocked Thea out of the chalk circle, she spun, sweeping out her staff to hit her opponent on the wrist, then twirling around to hit him on the side of the knee.

"Two hits! Jensen out. Win to Thea!" The Dragon Rider clapped again, and this time we all stood up and cheered. Thea had won the duel challenge, and I was happy that she looked so pleased with herself.

I was also happy the instructors called for a short break. The sun passed the mid-day mark and we were sent onto the less physical challenges. Tables were brought out and placed along one side of the training ground while overhead a huge, shielding flag was attached to the walls to protect everyone from the heat of the day.

First up was dragon-spotting. We were separated out individually and each given a piece of paper, quill and ink. I was dreading this test because my writing wasn't the best, but Merik had said you didn't have to be the best speller to be a Dragon Rider, just a good reader. Thanks to my ma, that I could do.

Across from us, a patch of wall was kept uncovered and shone brilliantly in the sun. Far above, one of the adjudicators hoisted a piece of board, roughly cut into the shape of a dragon. It cast a perfect shadow down on the wall.

That's easy, a short-necked forest green, I thought, writing down the words. It appeared obvious to me because the neck to body ratio was small, and the creature was stocky.

Next I saw a long, sinuous barbed tail with wings that fanned out to fine points.

Got to be a blue of some kind. They generally liked colder places and they have those long wings to help them glide over the snow. I tapped the writing feather against my chin. Aha! A blue stealer!

The challenge progressed, different silhouettes being displayed faster now. I thought I was doing well, but maybe I was just getting it all wrong. We went through all of the more common species: the small white, the double-tooth black, the marsh green, four-winged ossifer.

The last was one that had Thea excitedly leaning her head down as soon as the shadow appeared on the wall. A crimson red—our dragon. I still didn't know her name yet. I wondered about my score, and about dragon names, while handing my paper to the instructor and waiting for the results to be read out.

"First place, with ten correct answers, trainee Syl!" the commander read out, making me stamp the ground in exasperation. What did I get wrong?

"With nine correct answers, trainee Smith!" My exasperation evaporated as a wave of disbelief and happiness rushed over me. I turned to see Thea nodding encouragingly. I thought my heart would burst.

Next came Merik, then Beris and Thea in joint fourth, followed by Shakasta and the others. I had done well. Very well! Now I was glad I had stuck with it during those hard first days. I might not ever be first at all things, but my fears of being last in all tests were now banished.

"Trainees, you will perform, one at a time, a map challenge," the commander called out. Long, cylindrical pots stoppered and filled with bits of papyrus were put onto the tables. The commander looked us over. "We will set a sand clock running. When we sound the horn, you must try to identify and track the clues from one map to another, leading you to solve the mystery of where a missing dragon and its riders might be. You will be judged as to how long it takes you! Each challenge is different, so do not think you can succeed by copying the efforts of another."

Butterflies swarmed in my stomach like young dragons, but Merik gave me a thumbs up.

Names were draw one at a time. Each time the Dragon Horn blew another trainee ran to the table. Two ran out of time before they could finish. And then my name was called. My hands chilled and sweat popped on my lip. The horn blew loud enough that it seemed to shake my bones. I ran to the tables to start on the first map.

This one was easy. It was a map of Mount Hammal with a list

of codes and annotations along one side. I read down the list quickly.

Red flag in a circular pattern meant a general warning, and green flag for forest. A missing dragon was last seen flying north. Looking at the map these clues meant that I was looking for a forest directly north of the enclosure. There were the woods on the side of the mountain itself, but I rather doubted any dragon and its riders would get lost only a few miles from home.

Checking the map, I scanned for the next nearest forest.

There…Wynchwood. I took a ruler and drew a red line from Mount Hammal to the blob of colour that signified the unmarked Wynchwood forest to the north, then turned to the map tube, looking for a more detailed map of the region. I could find nothing that matched exactly, but an aerial map was close. Swathes of orange, reds and blues indicated the lay of the land. Again, I saw annotations on the side of the map. Three small banner-ribbons meant three dragon beats high in elevation. And the blue flag stood for water.

I searched the area. The three small banner ribbons I knew were like scarves that were added to the flag poles to indicate how high or low a feature was. One scarf-like ribbon meant about house height, two ribbons meant castle height, and three ribbons meant even higher.

That's quite a high elevation, I thought, frowning at my map.

There were no white patches of high mountains on this map…and what did the blue for water mean?

I scoured the different hills and dips of the forest until I saw a feature that might fit the bill. Eagle Falls? I'd heard of that place. It was supposed to be quite high. That could certainly make it 'high water.' I drew a red line to the area, then held up my hand and waited for a Dragon Rider to come to me.

"Yes, scrub?" he said, his voice stern.

I told him my findings, that I thought that the flags told me our dragon and its riders must have travelled to Eagle Falls, in Wynchwood Forest.

He nodded. "As you and your team search the falls, you find the downed dragon has taken ill. The riders tell you there is a rare herb that is not stocked at Mount Hammal that can heal the dragon. You must retrieve this rare herb that only grows in beech trees just below the snowline."

Herb. Beech. Under the snowline.

I nodded and turned to the map tube for a much larger map of the surrounding area. I found an elevation map that showed the white patches of the highest mountains, but they didn't say what type of trees grew where.

I turned to a smaller, land map for the different shapes of tree drawings and found several woods that must be beech a few hours away by dragon. But beech didn't grow that high up. I didn't know what to think. I couldn't find beech that fit the description of living near the snowline. I scanned the woods, but no, each stand of trees seemed to be in the valleys and nowhere near the hills.

What would make a cold place hot enough for beech trees? I thought. Don't follow the woods…look for the current maps!

Rummaging through the map canister, I found what I was looking for, a strange sort of map with place names written along the sides and arrows pointing all directions. I knew from my time in the map room these arrows were air currents, either blowing down from the cold north or up from the warm south.

By laying the names over the elevation map, I could track where the cold air flowed down one side of the Leviathan Mountains and out into the foothills. There was only one place where an arrow of warmer southern air crept along a wide river gulf, pooling into an area surrounded by frost-bitten hills.

By going back to the land map, I shouted out when I saw that yes, right there on that seemingly high altitude spot, there was a stand of beech. "There!" I shouted, looking up to the Dragon Rider.

"Well done," he said, raising a gloved hand to indicate a trainee had completed the task.

I heard scattered gasps and glanced at the sand clock. Only a small sliver of sand had passed through to the bottom—yet I had solved the puzzle.

Striding back to my bench, I waited in silence, trying to ignore Merik pulling happy faces. He finished next, with a time as good as my own. Wil and then Thea and Shakasta pretty much tied, barely finishing. Beris took a few minutes longer, eventually slamming his fist on the spot where the herb must be, and just before time ran out.

Thea looked crestfallen as she walked back to her bench. She hadn't done so well this afternoon at all, but I didn't know how to make her feel better.

Commander Hegarty stood before us again. "Trainees! Thank you for your efforts. I and my fellow adjudicators will retire to discuss everything we have seen today and return with our verdicts." Relief washed through me. It was done, no matter what else, it was over. All the students split into groups, talking over the day. The tests were being cleared and banqueting tables were being brought out.

I waited at the edge of the group, trying to catch Thea's eye. When I finally caught up to her, I grinned. "Thea! Well done!"

She was dragging her feet at the back of the group, looking glum. "Well done for what?" she barked. "I did terribly! My father will be so disappointed. I...I won't make it."

"Terrible? What are you talking about? You did great beating Jensen in the duels. Or how about how you did in the race?"

Her face stayed set, her mouth pulled down and her eyes dull. She shook her head. "Thanks Seb, it's just...I need to be better than good. I'm a Flamma, and the House of Flamma has always produced the best Dragon Riders. I can't fail that—I can't have others seeing me a failure. I...I've got to make through training."

"Well, I see you as a Dragon Rider," I told her. She looked at sideways, her frown turning puzzled.

Before I could say anything else, Merik crashed into me. "Well done, Sebastian! You were great! I've never seen anyone complete the map challenge so fast." He clapped me on the shoulder, offering me a pork sandwich he had grabbed off the tables from where food was being brought out.

I broke it in half, turning to offer half to Thea, but she was already gone.

I don't think anything will make her happy. I turned away from where she had been, and I was still left wondering if we would ever make a team.

CHAPTER 9

DRAGON RIDERS

I knew Seb was only trying to make me feel better, but I couldn't bear to be around anyone so cheery right now. The golden Dragon Horn blew for what was probably the last time that day and it made me feel sick. I stood up from where I had been sitting on a low bench just around the corner from the others and on the edge of the archery yard. I walked heavily back to the training area. It had been a couple of hours since the commander, the other instructors, and the Dragon Riders and had gone into their meeting to decide our fates, leaving us trainees to fight over the food and wait and wait…and…wait.

I wanted to kick myself for failing—and kick Seb for making me feel like he was just being stupid. He didn't get how the world worked at all.

I'm a girl. A Lady, in fact! I kicked a stone, heard it thock against one of the walls. I had grown up listening to my brothers talk about flying lessons and fighting bandits and sharing tales about derring-do with Prince Justin. I didn't want to lose my chance at all of that. I had thought Seb would be the obstacle in my way. Instead, I'd been my own enemy.

I let out an exasperated growl and joined the others. The

banqueting tables had been cleared away. The kitchen cooks were washing pewter plates and mugs in large, steaming barrels of water heated from deep within Mount Hammal. A wooden platform and stage had just been hastily erected across one side of the training area.

Large golden, red, green and blue banners hung down on the sides of the stage with the emblems of the Dragon Academy stitched on in vibrant colours. Along the stone palisade wall I could see all the Dragon Riders in their official uniforms, their helmets of swept-back horns standing to attention, their armor gleaming as they awaited the appointing ceremony. This would be the moment when we found out what our roles would eventually be.

And I would find out I had failed.

The chance for a woman to be a Dragon Rider was rare enough, but I had wanted to make my father proud. I had wanted others to see me as someone who deserved to be here because of my skills.

I sighed. I was okay with dueling and fighting since that was all fairly natural to me. But I was really annoyed about the map challenges and not doing well with dragon identification. I should have been better, because I was supposed to be the navigator. That was where the other female riders that I knew of had been assigned. If I couldn't even do that well…

"Hey, Thea!" Sebastian was heading over to stand at my side.

I smiled thinly at him. "I didn't know you were so good at maps." I didn't realize until the words were out of my mouth just how harsh they must sound.

Seb looked hurt, but he just shrugged. "It's just a natural thing for me." He sounded uneasy as if he expected me to hit him with a staff or something. "I wasn't holding out on you or anything."

I nodded, feeling foolish. He had echoed my thoughts exactly, and I could see he wasn't trying to show me up at all. He was too good-hearted for that. "Never mind. I know. I meant to say…well done. You were really good." Seb smiled, all trace of hurt completely forgotten.

How can he do that? Just forget all the bad stuff? He was going to be a protector! He had to be tough. Before I could tell him that, Commander Hegarty ascended the steps of the stage. My brain stopped arguing with itself and just froze.

The top-ranking Dragon Riders, my brothers Reynalt and Ryan amongst them, also stepped onto the stage. And Prince Justin. Heat washed through me. He must have seen how badly I had embarrassed myself. My mouth suddenly went dry and my heart beat a little faster. But Prince Justin just gave me a grin and a small wave. Strangely, I felt immediately better. He didn't seem to think I was stupid and a total failure. I thought he might actually like me, but why did I care about that?

"Trainees of the Dragon Academy," Commander Hegarty roared. "Welcome to your appointing ceremony. We will call out your names and your positions and you will also meet with your dragon, who will approve of the match."

I braced myself. Now everyone would find out I had failed my family—and my dragon. And Seb, too.

"First! Beris,—protector. His navigator is Syl." A roar rose up as their stocky blue dragon landed on the platform overhead. The two boys marched up onto the stage, accepting their badges to show that they had moved from scrubs to cadets. They turned to their dragon, climbed the stairs. The blue nosed at each of them in turn. After a few seconds, the dragon roared and was directed back to the enclosure by the other Dragon Riders. Beris and Syl joined those Dragon Riders standing atop the palisades. They were now on their way to becoming riders.

"Jensen as protector with Wil as navigator," Commander Hegarty called out. He waited. A hissing and a flap of wings preceded a green that landed on the platform to bless the partnership. Will and Jensen got their badges, went to greet their dragon, and joined the Dragon Riders, cadets now too.

I gulped and waited for our turn.

"Agathea as protector, and Sebastian navigator," the commander said.

I could only stare at him, stunned, unable to move. I'm a protector? But girls were never protectors. Even Varla, the other female cadet, was in training to be a navigator. Seb grabbed my arm. I stumbled forward with him. I could hear a ripple of amazement from the others.

We walked up the steps and onto the stage, bowed to the commander, who pinned a badge with a sword and a pair of wings on my leather jerkin and then a badge with an arrow and a pair of wings on Seb.

We turned, and Seb pulled at my sleeve. "Look, there she is." I looked up to see our red uncoiling above us, landing as light as a beam of light on the platform and chirruping at both of us.

Seb ran up the stairs. I followed. He walked up to her without hesitation, holding out his hand for her to bump her nose against it. I approached a little slower, still unable to believe what had just happened. The dragon enthusiastically snuffed my clothes, as if wondering if I had treats for it or wanting to know about my badge.

I was a protector.

Standing by the side of our red, wondering at her size and power, I felt something pass over me, like a wave of dizziness. Turning, I could see that whatever had just happened to me was connected to Seb and the dragon. Seb opened his eyes and his mouth, grinning as if amazed at a funny joke, but then our dragon was roaring and leaping high into air, heading back to the enclosure.

"This way," one of the other Dragon Riders said. He led us over to stand beside Jensen and Wil. He handed us each a helmet made of leather to signify we had become cadets at the academy. Below us, Commander Hegarty read out the next names.

"What was all that about?" I hissed out of the corner of my mouth at Sebastian. He looked open-mouthed and stupid.

"Her name. She told me her name," Sebastian hissed back at me.

"What?" I said, almost not believing it. But I couldn't forget that strange shiver of feeling that had passed over me. Something had happened…but the dragon had talked to him? I'd heard tales of that…I just hadn't believed them. I'd thought they were like the stories of the Darkening—just tales. I shivered.

"Kalax," Seb said. Another second shiver went over me, for somehow I knew that he was right.

Kalax. Our dragon's name is Kalax. And I was going to be a Dragon Rider.

Chapter 10
Flying Lessons

Over the next few weeks, I tried to keep my head down and work hard at my new role as a protector. I got a bit of teasing from Beris and Shakasta, which I would usually have brushed off. But I couldn't.

I was irritable and annoyed. I felt awkward and clumsy, like everyone was looking at me just because I was a girl. I was a weirdo. A worse misfit than Seb. A girl protector? Who had ever heard of such a thing?

I could just imagine the others, laughing at me behind my back. What if Prince Justin was laughing at me, too? Maybe I was already the talk of the royal court. What would my father think? And I could just see my mother's face crumple when she heard her daughter was to be a protector—and now must fight just like a man.

A fact that made it slightly worse was that the navigators were taken off to work with the dragons to 'develop a connection' or so the commander called it. From what I had seen so far, Seb already had a pretty good connection going already. I was jealous of him—he got time with our dragon.

That left me with Jensen, Beris, Shakasta and the other

protector cadets—there were three more of them, boys I didn't know very well. We alternated our days between dueling and riding 'dragons'. Not real dragons, but large, wicker baskets hung suspended from the ceiling on ropes and placed on the end of giant seesaws. We jostled around, leaning this way and that, trying to stay in the saddle as other riders managed the pulley systems, tossing us around as we reached for our bows and arrows to fire at targets.

And then there was the flag system.

Oh, by my dragon's fire! There were so many. We drilled relentlessly, the instructors yelling out an order that we had to transmit to another dragon or a tower. We were judged on how fast we could yank out the red or the green or the blue flag and wave it high enough for someone else to see. Despite what Seb had been trying to teach me, it was a nightmare.

"At least you're not a navigator," Beris said under his breath. I had taken off my sweaty helmet, finished from our most recent fake-dragon ride. I smiled at him. I knew he was only trying to be funny, but he came off as mean. I would have hit him, but I knew my temper wasn't doing much better. He was becoming one of those who thought he could force others to look up to him. My brothers had gone through a phase like this, and I hoped this would pass quickly for Beris.

"Least you're not trying to wrestle dragons, huh? Bet Seb's

been eaten up by now." Beris laughed, and I shook my head and moved away.

Cadet training was a pain, but I couldn't deny that it was also fun. Every time we came to the end of another day of dueling and waving flags and clinging onto saddles there also came the moment I cherished the most. I was tired, the sun was fading over the battlements and my body was still warm from all of the day's exertions. I sat down on one of the wooden benches, my mind gloriously blank. I watched Beris, Jensen and the others wearily walking across the arena. I felt at peace.

I liked this moment because it was one of the few times that I could relax and remember where I was and what I was doing. The high walls of the academy rose around me, cocooning me into its own little world. The sky was purpling above as the sun headed for its bed. I looked up to see a flight of dragons pass by overhead. Was one of my brothers up there, looking down?

It was at this time of the day when I could think that I would be up there soon. I, Agathea Flamma, would train hard, and when I graduated I would be a proper Dragon Rider. Despite all of the bruises and the aches and sprains, it still didn't seem real, even now, to think that I would join the list of Dragon Riders that stretched back for generations in my family.

"Feeling good?" A voice startled me out of my reverie. I look up to see Commander Hegarty, pausing as he walked up to the battlements.

I jumped up. "Sorry, Commander, sir. Just getting my breath back."

"No, you carry on, Thea." Hegarty crooked a smile at me. "I've noticed you take some time to pause at the end of the day, which is good. I do the same. I have to walk the palisade walls to look out at Torvald and the enclosure, realize what all of this is all about."

"What it's all about," I repeated the words. I nodded as I agreed. But all the while I was feeling as always when I spoke to the commander—I didn't one hundred percent understand what he was trying to tell me.

Hegarty barked a laugh. I blushed, certain he could see right through me to my deepest thoughts. "It's about trust, wonder and protection, cadet. I thought you'd understood that by now. Trusting your partner, trusting your dragon…and trusting yourself. It's the trust that allows you to be here in the first place, and allows you to have wonder."

"Wonder?" I asked.

"Yes. We are in the business of riding dragons. What is more wondrous than that? We have a history that stretches back almost five hundred years—back to the time of the Darkening and more. Just think on that. Hundreds of years of humans and dragons working together, bringing peace and justice to the world." The commander's face went from his usual dry humor to one of rapt wonder. "What we're doing is a thing of myth, cadet. And the people of Torvald and King Durance's line trust us to protect them."

"From everything." I shivered as I thought of the story I had once heard of the Darkening. It didn't matter to me if it was true—just that it meant a Dragon Rider would go up against anything. Including something as vague and terrifying as utter darkness.

The commander nodded and glanced up at the sky. "We're here to do something that people haven't ever thought to do in the whole history of the world—we bring harmony. We protect those who are less fortunate, less powerful than us, because that is what you do when you have strength and power on your side."

I almost asked him about the Darkening—if it was a true tale. But I didn't want to seem like a child who needed bedtime stories. I felt the rightness of his words in my gut, and this time when I nodded, I did so more than believing it, but feeling it.

Hegarty nodded at me. "Don't worry, Agathea. I think you'll do just fine."

But I wondered—what would I do if…when I had to go up against a real enemy?

*   *   *

A month into cadet training and finally I was going to get my first chance to ride Kalax. Sebastian was more than excited about this day. As soon as I was awake and dressed, he came and found me, his hands waving all over the place. "She's so gentle. She's great. You won't feel anything like it, it's like being alive!"

"You already are alive," I said, a little sternly. He laughed, but I hadn't meant it as a joke.

"Wait until you're up there. You'll see. She's so funny as well. Naughty, you know," he was saying enthusiastically.

"Are you always going to be this cheery so early in the morning?" I said to him, growling a bit.

His smile faded and he quieted. "I just wanted to encourage you," he muttered.

Since there were two girls training, I shared a room with Varla, but I never saw much of her. She'd been here longer than five years, and she was training to be a navigator, so she trained with navigators. Her protector, Ty, right now was recovering from a broken leg—he'd fallen from his dragon on one of their flights. Also, Varla didn't seem to like me much—maybe because she'd been a cadet for so long and had yet to graduate. I didn't know if that was her fault, or her protector's or her dragon's. I didn't care. I was here to become a rider.

100

I followed Seb out of the keep and up the stairs to the platforms where all the cadet dragons were at their assigned ports, blowing little puffs of smoke or flames into the morning air. Jensen's sinuous green hissed and appeared skittish around the others, and Beris' blue flapped its wings loudly, like the crack of a whip.

"That's a dominance display," Sebastian said, pointing out the blue's behavior.

"Then why isn't Kalax...displaying back?" I pointed to our red who sat on its haunches, cleaning its front feet and claws.

"She's ignoring the others. Showing them all that she doesn't care." Seb beamed like a new father. I shook my head—him and his fancies over our red.

We headed up to see giant tandem saddles atop each dragon's back. Sebastian would be up front, with me at the back. He scampered on more easily than I would have expected. He soon had attached the clips and buckles to strap himself into his harness, his helmet sat slightly wonky on his head.

I stared at the saddle. At last I found the rounded stirrup strap and used it to climb up onto the back of the dragon. The saddle was all polished leather with straps that fixed our legs into place. The saddles had a pulley and gear system that we could use to signal our dragons and steer. My saddle had fewer controls than Sebastian's. Instead, it had weapon belts and saddle bags stacked behind and to the sides of my seat. I was the protector, after all.

Once in the saddle, I could feel the gentle rise and fall of Kalax's body beneath us as she breathed. A slight warm feeling from her body radiating upward. She smelled of soot dust and fresh pine somehow. I reminded myself I would have to ask Sebastian why she always smelled of fragrant wood.

Her scales were of different sizes, depending on where they were on her body. Some were the size of dinner plates, others just the size of my little fingernail. The largest scales overlapped with each other. Along her back the scales even started to fold and rise in the middle to a bony edge. It was miraculous how they all fitted together, moving as smooth and as softly as a piece of weaving.

"Ready?" one of the Dragon Riders shouted.

No! I didn't feel ready at all. I wanted to shout to wait, but already those Dragon Riders not going up were stepping down from the platforms. Seb was giving me a thumbs up.

The Dragon Horn blew, and one by one, the dragons launched themselves off the wooden platforms atop Mount Hammal. They looked like diving sea birds to me. I watched as Jensen's green and then Beris' blue appeared to fall off the edge. My heart flipped. Our turn was coming.

There was a lurch from underneath me. I realized we were

going. Kalax sprang as powerfully as a mountain cat over the edge. She wasn't unfolding her wings, but fell like a dart behind the others!

Sebastian gave a whoop, but I could only grip the pommel of my saddle. I remembered to pull down the goggles over my eyes just in time, before gripping the handles in front of me with my gauntlets, squeezing them until I thought my fingers would break.

The other dragons pulled out their wings, catching the rising thermals, suddenly shooting up into the sky at dazzling speeds.

But we weren't.

Below us, the ground and trees came roaring closer. Kalax held onto her dive. I could see the small crofts and buildings of the goat herders and woodsmen.

"Stop," I shouted. I could make out the individual goats on the sides of the hill, getting larger, larger now!

With a sound like a crack of lightning, Kalax threw her wings open. My stomach lurched as we caught the ground thermals and soared into the air, barreling past the other dragons due to our momentum.

Had I shouted? I couldn't remember. It was all I could do to keep a hold of the handles of my saddle. Kalax started to soar high, flapping her wings only rarely as she allowed the currents of the air to carry her.

"Thea? Okay back there?" Seb shouted to me. He half-turned and held up a hand to wave at me.

I tried to wave back, but found I couldn't take my hands off the controls. I kept seeing myself being dragged out of my seat, my harness breaking, sending me spinning down to splat on the ground.

"Thea?" Seb asked. He turned again and his expression showed he was clearly worried.

I must look terrible. He can probably see how pale I am. It felt as if all my blood had rushed to my feet. I nodded, forcing a grin that probably didn't fool him. Seb frowned. Leaning forward, he put his hands onto the scales of the dragon's side.

Don't do that! I thought. His balance seemed precarious, leaning like that, thousands of feet up in the air. But then there was that strange sensation of feeling passing through him and the dragon. With barely a twitch of the dragon's wings, the ride got smoother.

Did he just tell her to do that? I gaped, looking between Seb and Kalax in astonishment.

All it had taken for Kalax to fly smoother was a slight change in the way she held her wings and how she angled her tail. Her tail acted like a rudder on a ship, steering and slowing her, or driving us in a powerful turn. With a careful rise of one wing, we started to slowly turn in a majestic, elegant movement.

"Don't be scared!" Seb grinned. "Trust her. Kalax knows what she's doing." He thought for a moment, before adding, "Sort of."

"Great. That doesn't exactly fill me with confidence," I yelled at him.

"Here, try this. Feel the dragon underneath you," Seb shouted over to me, his voice carrying. Up here, there was little sound other than the flap of dragon wing and our dragon's breathing. We were one with the wind, riding its currents. The ground was a patchwork of fields and woods stitched together by roads and rivers.

"No, feel her in your gut. How big she is, how strong she is," Seb was saying.

I tried, closing my eyes just to shut him up. I could feel the warmth of her emanating upwards and the solidity of her form. Seb was right, it was quite reassuring.

"Now try to find her heartbeat," he said.

I concentrated on the dragon underneath me. I almost could feel something—a distinct powerful, rhythmic shudder that went through her body and into mine, travelling up my legs. Her heartbeat seemed to match mine.

"Reach out to her, not with your hands but inside," Seb was saying.

I opened my eyes a crack to see he was sitting with his hands not on the handles, but raised in the air, just letting his legs and Kalax do the flying.

He's mad. This is some weird navigator trick.

But when I closed my eyes, I could feel the warm, rhythmical beat of her heart filling me with strength. I breathed out, feeling as though I wasn't actually myself but that the dragon and I were both part of one thing, our heartbeats matching perfectly and our breaths the same.

"You're doing it," Seb cried. I opened my eyes to realize that somewhere in my meditation, I had released my terrified grip. I sat with my arms held out wide, as if they were wings of my own to match hers.

Thea, a voice said in my mind. It was a large, feminine voice, both playful and inquisitive.

"By the First…?" I slammed back into my body and seized the handles on my saddle once more.

"You heard her? You heard Kalax, didn't you?" Seb was grinning and patting the side of the dragon.

I didn't know what I had heard—and I didn't want to know. It scared me a little.

"Not many people can do that. Some navigators, apparently. If they have a close connection." Seb was still grinning. "I've been told I can teach you the connection, but you've got to let me do most of the guiding, as we don't want to confuse poor Kalax with too many orders."

I was content to remain firmly in my own body and let Seb have his 'magic connection.' At least for now. As we flew back to the enclosure, I could feel once again the solid certainty and reassuring presence of Kalax. I guessed she was amused.

We landed easily back on the platform. Kalax fluttered her wings, seeming a little off-balance as if she was trying to get the handle of landing with a harness and two riders. She gave a little sloppy hop, but Seb was cooing and purring to her.

"Don't worry, you can do it. That's great. Perfect," he was saying.

I unclipped my belt and harness and jumped out of the saddle to land on firm wood.

I looked up to see Beris standing in front of the platform. "How was that then, oh mighty warrior?" He looked from me to Seb. The tone in Beris' voice annoyed me and the weird connection I had felt with the dragon had upset me more than I had first thought. If I were a navigator, I would have that connection—except I wasn't sure I really wanted another mind in mine. More confused feelings cluttered my head. I was proud to be a protector. But all my childish daydreams of being a rider had been of me as a navigator, because that was the only position I thought acceptable. Nothing was turning out how I had dreamed it to be.

"By the first breath of fire, what is your partner doing to that poor dragon? He can't marry the thing, you know!" Beris said and grinned.

I winced. Beris was a fool, but he was right in one way. Seb was embarrassing—himself and me. This wasn't a nursery, and dragons weren't big, cuddly puppies. We were in the king's service. We were in training to be strong warriors. My partner was humiliating me. But I only gave Beris a flat stare and crossed my arms.

Shaking his head, Beris waved a hand. "Some of us are going down to the Troll's Head later, but…" he nodded in Seb's direction. "Don't bring him." He turned and left. Seb dismounted from Kalax, and he was chirruping at her like she was a pet parrot.

"What did you think, Thea? She's great, isn't she?" Seb asked.

"Yeah. Great. Look, thank you for that. Very informative." I tried to insert a bit of stiff gravity to my voice. I had to be the best. We were the realm's own defense, after all. "I'll be going out tonight with the others, Beris and the rest. The place is for officers and nobles only, really. You…you may want to work on your manners before you even think of showing your face." I wanted to make it clear he had embarrassed me—that he needed to learn how to act like a Dragon Rider.

Seb frowned. He opened and closed his mouth. His usually meek expression twisted, and guilt stabbed into my gut. Those feelings turned into a flash of annoyance that must have shown on my face—he had caused all of this by acting like a child in front of Beris.

Seb straightened. "I see. Of course." He turned back to Kalax, patting her side and starting to unfix her harness straps.

It took everything in me, every bit of annoyance and remembering that Seb needed to learn. He had to learn. He has to toughen up and remember that we're soldiers. "We're not pet handlers," I told him, keeping my voice gruff. Seb and Kalax both put their heads to one side as if I was the crazy one here.

Annoyed, I stalked off to get washed and changed. And I tried not to feel two stares stuck on my back.

CHAPTER 11

RUMORS

It made me mad to watch Thea walk off with her nose in the air and Beris, Shakasta and the rest waiting for her. Noble brats. I was feeling hurt, I knew. After everything that I had tried to teach Thea, she was still doing her best to treat me like any other peasant.

Which I guess I am—a blacksmith's kid in an expensive uniform.

A chirrup from behind me had me turning. Kalax had sensed my unease and was looking between me and the retreating back of Thea anxiously. She doesn't get it. Looking at the confusion that rippled through the air and in the way that Kalax was holding her wings, I knew I needed to comfort her.

"It's okay, Kalax." Reaching out, I stroked the sensitive skin around her nose. "It's okay. Me and Thea, we aren't enemies, we just…we argue every now and again. We change and then get back to normal."

I got a strong mental image of Jensen's sinuous, slinky green dragon rearing up on its hind legs, hissing at me—or at Kalax—over a half-carcass of deer, growling in the back of his throat.

"Yes, Kalax, that's right. It's like that. Just friends falling out every now and again. No need to worry." I hushed at her, taking the heavy bristled brush from the side of the platform to brush down her scales. She purred in the back of her gullet—a quiet, reassuring roar. After a few minutes of this, she was ready to return to the enclosure where she had a den in the side of the crater—a small cavern with a bed of straw.

"And you keep away from that green," I warned her. She answered by coughing a small puff of flame into the air.

"Yes, I'm sure you would. Now go on with you." I grinned, momentarily cheered up by the straightforward, cheerful way Kalax thought.

It was strange. Did the other navigators have this sort of connection with their dragons? Did Syl? Or Wil? Over the last few weeks, the more time that I spent with Kalax, the more it was like I could read her moods and thoughts. Only recently had I started seeing things I knew could only come from the dragon. She was communicating with me through the power of her mind. It felt right and natural, but I didn't like to talk to anyone about it. Even Thea hadn't understood.

I'll have to try and hide any of my hurt feelings about Thea away from Kalax, I thought, trudging back to the dormitory to get changed. It would only confuse the dragon, especially when she was learning how to sense Thea's thoughts.

I flung off my training clothes and putting on the tunic I'd been given when I'd first arrived at the academy. Over this, I put on a warm woolen cloak.

I headed for the kitchen, and then made for the main gates and the path that wound down the mountain and into the city.

*   *   *

If Thea was going to head out of the academy, I wasn't going to stay there alone. The city appeared strange to my eyes after spending so much time at the academy. It seemed both bigger from the street—crowded, noisy and full of people. Yet also much, much smaller. I remember looking down as I soared over it on Kalax's broad back and wondering how all those people were stuffed into such a little space.

The city of Torvald had been built in a series of semi-circular layers, extending up and down the Hammal Mountain range. My old district—one of the poorest—stood almost at the very bottom, near the bridge and the gate where the woodsmen entered the city. There were very few flat areas in the city, aside from inside the buildings. All the cobbled streets sloped downward, twisting and turning as they cut their way around the land.

All the buildings had been made of stone. More stones formed the gates and walls, and the mountain streams had been cut and channeled into fountains and decorative parks. The city was highly segmented with different districts walled off from each other. The nobles and the palace lived at the highest end of the city, while those in trades and the guild-houses stood below them, and then more markets below that.

And Monger's Lane right over there at the bottom.

I crossed the main avenues, avoiding the crowds of people who were out in the early evening. Mostly they were revelers, but a few of the city watch walked the streets with their lanterns and red cloaks.

The streets grew narrower and more crowded as I made my way to Monger's Lane. A few people sat outside their homes and businesses on small benches, puffing on their pipes and enjoying the evening air. There was still a touch of warmth from the day, but the stars were coming out and I could tell it would be chilly later. Under my arm, I carried a basket of stuffed loaves, a half roll of cheese and a pot of the pickled vegetables that I knew my mom had always liked. The cook at the academy, Margaret, had made up the basket for me when I'd told her I was heading home for the evening. I had asked for just a little something for myself. Like me, she was from the poorer parts of the city. She knew what a difference a bit of fine food could make, so she sent me on my way with a feast to share.

I passed in front of the Orc's Breath, one of the taverns at the head of the lane. My father frequented the place. I ducked past it, hearing the noise of raucous singing and laughter spilling through the open door.

Moving too fast, I tripped on the cobbles, and just managing to put my hand out to catch myself before the basket got smashed. The roll of cheese, however, bounced out of the basket and down one of the alleys. Quickly, I ran after it, picking it up just as I heard voices from two men who had stepped out of the Orc's Breath. They were dressed in the heavy leather jerkins and breeches of woodsmen, and they spoke with the rough accent of men from the north.

"...war? Nah, mate, you must be mad."

"No—I tell you, something is brewing up there in the north, something bad. I've men now who won't go into the northern woods to cut. Cursed they call it. They come back last time out with stories of starting to forget paths they've walked since they were boys."

The two men weren't drunk. I knew that from years of avoiding a loud, drunken and quick-tempered father. I started to turn away, but then the first man said, "Dragons. We got the Dragon Riders. No one will raise a sword against Torvald because of them."

"This is something else. It's not just my own lads talking. I heard it from a merchant who travels up and down the Leviathan Mountains. He meets traders from all over, even from beyond the mountains, coming over the sea. He says some of the tribes up that way are telling tales of whole villages disappearing, people vanishing. Folks are moving away from danger and bringing the stories with them. It's the Darkening come back, some say."

I moved closer to hear more.

The second man gave a snort. "Tall tales, those old legends. Just old, scare-stories that travelers tell each other to keep the nights interesting. Villages vanishing, my eye. You're letting your lads lead you by the nose because they don't want to work—that's all. Come on, let's find another drink or two." Their voices faded as they headed down the lane.

War? Were we going to war? I repacked the basket and hurried to my old house. I knew my father would be out at one of the taverns, so I could have a few pleasant hours with my step-mother and sister if she was to home. I'd be able to give them a good meal and tell them about the academy.

But my mind wouldn't leave the tricky subject of war alone. Torvald hadn't been involved in a war for generations. And what of this talk of the Darkening? I'd heard some mention of such a thing—a child's story. But my father didn't hold with fanciful tales and the like. If he'd ever caught me so much as trying to listen to one of the old tales, told at the taverns or under the trees on a summer eve, he'd always clipped my ear and dragged me home. So maybe this was just travelers' tales. After all, the Dragon Riders were famous throughout the known realms. No one dared raise their armies against us.

But what if that is all going to change? My heart was troubled despite the warm welcome I had received at home.

CHAPTER 12

THE TRICK

The next day, I returned the basket to the academy kitchens and told Margaret just how much my step-mother and sister had liked her food. She waved me out of her domain with a cloth, telling me not to talk about it. "Don't want folk to think they'll all get free meals," she said, her voice cross.

The sun hadn't crested the palisade walls yet, but I could hear the early-morning croak of waking dragons from the enclosure. It was still early, a bright, sunny day with clear, blue skies above. I still had a little time before cadet training began and decided to walk up to the walls to look down on the enclosure and try to spot Kalax.

I was walking over when I heard a voice call my name. "Seb! Seb!" I turned to see Beris, huffing toward me, his hair still wet from his morning bath.

"Beris?" I gave him a nod and stiffened. I didn't have any problem with him, but I eyed him warily. I did not want to be the butt of some stupid joke.

"Sebastian, Thea she said that she wanted to go over some training or another with you, out by Hammal Lake. I meant to tell you last night, but you know, I must have forgot."

Because you were drunk when you got back, or maybe just didn't bother to tell me so I would be late.

"Hammal Lake? It's a bit of a way, isn't it? We've got flight practice in an hour." The cold-water lake was on the other side of the mountain, just lower than the peak itself where it caught the water from several small mountain streams before diverting it down into the city below. It was a nice, peaceful spot and the dragons occasionally fished the lake.

"Yeah—I know, crazy—but there's horses at the stables, you can always borrow one and get out there. She'll be waiting," Beris said, turning to walk away from me.

I didn't trust Beris, but I also knew it would be like Thea to be up early to try and do something no one else had done. Just to be sure, I went to look for her and couldn't find any sign of her at the academy. If I hurried now, I could just make it to the lake and back. I wasn't a very good rider, but the ponies were all sturdy and easy to ride. Making my way over to the stables, I checked out a small white and tan pony by the name of Bill. The tough little mountain ponies were kept for the moving of luggage and supplies to the academy. Fixing Bill up with a saddle, I rode out of the front gates as fast as I dared. These little mountain ponies didn't gallop as fast as the war stallions the knights of Torvald rode, but they were quicker and much more agile on the mountain paths.

The path to Hammal Lake was well-trod. It didn't take long before I crested the high ridge of the mountain. The clear blue waters of the lake glittered below, its shores dotted with shrubby hawthorn and pine trees.

The air was still cold, so I pulled my cloak tighter around me and urged the pony a little faster as we made our way back down the slope of boulders and ravines on the other side of the crest. I heard the cry of a kestrel flying over the bits of wild land beyond.

This place was beautiful and I could see why Thea might want to come out here on a morning such as this. I pulled in a breath, reveling in the fresh air and the feel of the wind against my hair. As I neared the path to the lakeside, I slowed Bill and started to search for signs of Thea and her pony.

"Thea?" I called out. My voice bounced off the high walls of a cliff, coming back to me muted and ghostly. I swung off the pony to climb a large bolder. From there I'd be able to see the entire lake shore. Bill put his head down to explore a bit of tough meadow grass. I couldn't see any sign of anyone being near—no tracks or anything. I started to wonder if she might have fallen in. A sudden twist tightened my stomach. Thea was a good swimmer, but the waters of Hammal Lake were deep and icy cold.

I climbed up higher, hoping to get some glimpse. I was starting to get worried as I crested the very top of the boulders and looked around.

"Thea? Thea!" The only answer was the caw of crows and the bleat of a few adventurous mountain goats.

A suspicion started to grow. Had I got here too late? Had she already gone back to the academy?

I decided to leave. If fitness-obsessed Agathea Flamma wanted to train out here, she could. I was going back. But when I returned to the spot where the pony had been, he wasn't there.

The sudden truth hit me.

Beris.

He'd followed me out here, stole my pony and left me abandoned. It was some cruel trick because he disliked how I'd beaten him in the selection trials.

I looked up at the ridge, seeing the sun flare and glare over it. It would take me hours to get back to the academy on foot. I would well and truly be late for flight practice. Thea wouldn't be able to ride Kalax without a second, and she would be grounded until I got back. And I might well be punished for this.

I sighed. Resentment knotted in my stomach. Head down, I started up the trail back to the academy.

CHAPTER 13

INSTRUCTOR MORDECAI

"Where in the heavens were you?" I glared at Seb. He'd walked back through the gates of the academy looking like he'd been on some kind of hike. Not only was he over an hour and a half late, but he wasn't even dressed for flight practice. He only had on his tunic, breeches and boots. His hair stood up as if he hadn't bothered to brush it.

I'd been waiting for Seb up on the platform when Beris and Shakasta had come by and told me no one had seen Seb this morning. Beris said that he'd heard a rumor that Seb had walked down to the poor districts of Torvald, to where the taverns flowed with cheap and strong liquor and people stayed up all through the night, making fools of themselves.

I glared at Seb. He shook his head and tried to wave me off, and I could see he was already coming up with excuses.

"Are you just ignoring everything I'm trying to teach you? What—you don't really care for me, for us? Or the academy! Everything that's been done for you, and you still…still act like this!" My face heated and I bit down on the rest of my words. The other cadets had been allowed to go up into the skies above the city where they were practicing formation flying—the very essence of a dragon-attack squadron!

"I thought you had really turned a corner at the selection trials. I thought that maybe, despite your low birth, there was a real Dragon Rider in there somewhere underneath all the dirt. But now you go and do something like this!"

Shaking my head, I looked away. The worst part of it was that last night Beris had told me that it was well known that Sebastian's dad was a drunkard. "The drunkard smith of Monger's Lane," Beris called him. Shakasta had said it was a marvel that anyone got any work out of the man, although his work was good when he was sober.

And I am stuck with that kind of man for a partner?

Seb stopped in front me, his shoulders slumping. "No, Thea, you don't understand. It wasn't me, it was Beris. He told me that you were at the lake."

"What?" I snapped. I narrowed my eyes, sure that must be a lie and a weak one at that. "By the First Dragon, why would I be down the lake at this time in the morning, especially as we have flight practice first thing?"

Seb stiffened. "As if you haven't been down by the lake, swimming on the coldest morning before. Or haven't been out running before dawn has even lightened the sky. Or haven't been up before everyone, at archery practice, or even… Oh, never mind. You just go on thinking whatever you want. Go hang out with Beris and Shakasta—you want to be their friend! I've got a stolen pony to find."

"Would that be this pony, cadet?" said a nasal, accusing voice getting louder.

Oh no—Instructor Mordecai.

Mordecai was the sort of man you never would expect to have ever been a Dragon Rider. Large and hunched over from shoulders that twisted his whole frame inwards, he looked more like a giant bug. His face was sallow and heavily wrinkled. His nose was a sharp hooked blade. Stringy grey hair fell from the sides of his head, wild in the morning breeze. Every cadet almost universally disliked him. The legend went that Mordecai had been a Dragon Rider some fifty years ago, but his dragon had become ill and died. His partner, unable take the loss of his dragon, had thrown himself off the observation tower, leaving Mordecai to grow bitter.

"Now you've really done it, Seb," I hissed at him. I turned to face the instructor who was stalking toward us, leading a mountain pony who was sweaty and caked with mud on his legs.

"You found him!" Seb blurted out, and then frowned.

I groaned inwardly.

"Found him, cadet?" Mordecai's eyes flashed. "He was

outside the stables, unsaddled, unbrushed, unfed and un-looked-after!" Mordecai's nostril's flared. "You know the rules, cadet. You tend to your animals, you tend to your duties. Anyone who cannot follow even the simplest of discipline and care does not deserve to be here!"

"But, sir—" Seb straightened and stuttered the words. I rammed an elbow into his side. There was no reasoning with Instructor Mordecai, and excuses just made him worse.

"Don't give me a story, cadet! There may come a time, if we are all incomparably unlucky, that you and your partner here are charged with defending Torvald, and during that time there may be many foes trying to deceive or trick you. Does that mean you will believe any tale? Or that you will just leave your dragon untended? Or abandon your partner?" He threw the horse brush that he held in his hand at Seb, who caught it awkwardly. "You and your partner rider share in the blame and share in the punishment. You will both tend to this poor beast, and then you will clean out the stables, and brush down every pony we have. When you are finished, then you may resume your flight practice!" he snapped.

"Thank you, Instructor Mordecai, we promise it won't happen again," I said quickly, before Sebastian could let out the frustration and anger I could see heating his skin.

Mordecai raised sharp eyes to look at me. He gave a

dismissive, snorting sound, then turned back to Seb. "Be thankful your partner understands the value of loyalty and duty, cadet. Learn from her." Mordecai stalked off, leaving the pony with us.

"Thanks," Seb said, his voice quiet as if he was too tired to argue.

Mouth pressed tight, I shook my head. I was still furious, but I wasn't sure if I was furious with him or just at the situation he had gotten us into. I didn't know if I should believe him when he said that Beris and the others had played a trick on him—but even if they had, what kind of idiot did that make him if they had?

"Come on," I said, trudging toward the stables. Seb picked up the pony's lead. I waved a hand at him. "You know we'll probably get marked down for this, don't you? That's one mark against us, and it means that we'll be stuck performing slow fly-bys over the city for the rest of our lives, or carrying post from one end of the city to another. That is, if we're lucky enough to graduate and not be sent down. We only get three chances to screw up—don't use up the other two!"

I turned away from him. A part of me was still frightened. What if the instructors began to think we couldn't care for our dragon? Would they even let us ride out on patrol? It wasn't unheard of for cadets to be dismissed from the academy—their dragon would be retired to the enclosure for breeding, and all of us would never fly together again. I couldn't think about that, but

I knew that I'd better keep a closer eye on Sebastian. He wasn't going to mess this up for me!

CHAPTER 14

THE GYPSIES OF DISTANT SHAAR

Disappointing Thea wasn't the worst of what I'd done—I was in trouble, and Thea was right about one thing. If either of us messed up more than three times, we'd both be thrown out. We'd lose Kalax, and Kalax would also lose her chance to fly. I knew this was a mark against me—the instructors wouldn't be happy that another cadet had played a trick, but I was even more at fault for having been caught by the lie. And I hated that.

Lying awake in my narrow bed and listening to the snores of the other boys in my room made me wary and sad. I couldn't trust anyone—not even Thea. Beris and Shakasta and Syl—they wanted me to fail. They would probably even be happy to see Thea have to leave with me since that just left more room for them to be the best.

I turned over and closed my eyes. It didn't help. Nothing did. Even flying with Kalax today—the first time we'd been in the air for days—had only managed to cheer me up a little bit.

I kept thinking about Thea, too. She was trying really hard to be the best Dragon Rider—I could see she was desperate to prove something to somebody, and I was just getting in the way. But I couldn't quit—if I failed, she did. No wonder she was so mad with me, still. She trained hard with me, but she wasn't smiling very much these days. It was all work and training and every now and then I would turn and see her watching me—as if she was afraid I was going to fail both her and Kalax.

Earlier today, I had heard Beris and the others sniggering about the drunkard of Monger's Lane. I'd tried to ignore them, but maybe that was what this was all about. Maybe I really didn't have any right to be here—maybe I was going to prove to be too like my da. If I went home, I could look after my step-mother and my sister, and I might be able to take over my da's smithy before he drank up all the profits.

But then Thea would never be a rider—and Kalax would never fly again with us.

Thumping my pillow, I tried to get to sleep, but I just couldn't. The look on Thea's face that I'd seen today, as if I had let her down again, kept haunting me. How could I even go out flying with her if she had no trust in me? Maybe it was already too late for us to make this work out.

I slipped from my bed, unable to sleep, and put on my old clothes—the ones I'd been wearing when Kalax had chosen me. The worn tunic and trousers felt comfortable— like I was wearing them instead of my cadet uniform which always left me feeling like the clothes were important but I wasn't.

I needed to get outside to where I could see the stars. I'd done this often enough back home, heading out into the hills and away from my da and the drinking and the stink of Monger's Lane. I could do some wandering and thinking—maybe this was what I'd been missing, being out under the stars where the sky seemed open and I could lie on the grass and watch the world spin.

It was easy to slip out of the academy. As cadets we weren't under as many rules as we had been as just trainees. And, in these long times of peace, there were hardly any guards kept on duty. Those few who walked the top of the stone walls liked to stay close to the fire in the braziers, warming their hands and talking softly to each other. I headed down the stone steps and out into the training yard. The world seemed quiet—even the chickens kept for the kitchen were asleep in their coop. I managed to sneak through the main gate, which stood open and unguarded. I headed down the lane without anyone even raising a word or turning a head toward the gate.

As soon as I got to the mountain lane, I stepped off the worn path and behind a boulder. A narrow track ran around the back of the city, wandering out past the craggy vineyards and the high meadows where sheep grazed. I didn't feel like climbing up to the ridge tonight, or of going down into the city itself. I felt curiously caught between the academy and the city, in a sort of no-man's-land, like I didn't belong to either anymore. I was a cadet, but maybe I'd fail at that. I was a smithy's son, but I wasn't that really, not anymore. So what was I?

The stars glittered overhead sharp as bits of glass, and the night animals called, hooted or barked as I walked the paths that wended past shepherds' huts and craggy orchards. The apples trees would be in blossom soon, and the chill in the night spoke of winter just past. From the hillside, I could look down into the broad, ornate gardens of the nobles' houses below and see lanterns sparkling. I turned away from that and kept walking.

The feeling soon stole over me that I wasn't alone. I slowed my step. Snippets of laughter drifted to me, and the smell of meat sizzling on a spit left my stomach growling. I hadn't been eating well these past few days.

The sound of a voice lifted up in song, accompanied by a fiddle. "…but by the long river, I will find my true love wa-i-ting!"

That's no noble's music, I thought. This was something much earthier. I followed the music to behind the orchards, where the high meadows opened out and the trees rose up around them, wild and untamable.

The rutted track led to a clearing underneath a rock face. The rock and the grass nearby glowed bright in the firelight. Edging closer, I saw a painted caravan with a curved roof and a pair of black and white draft horses tied to a line. Two men, a woman and two children stood or sat around the crackling fire that wove a pleasant smell of roast meat and wood smoke into the night.

They dressed—women and men and children—in bright, embroidered vests, black pants and boots, white shirts of a coarse weave, and slouch hats with tassels on the end.

Gypsies! I froze my steps. The traveling folk roamed the realms, not heeding any border and only rarely visiting any city. I hadn't thought they would ever camp this near to Mount Hammal and Torvald.

I'd met a few of the traveling folk over the years in Monger's Lane. The families would come up from the south every summer. The women of Monger's Lane bought herbs and spices from them, and they would trade for repairs to their wagons. Larger caravans sometimes came to the area to join in the autumn wood-chopping season, working away through winter with the foresters before moving on again in spring.

I thought about turning around to head back to the academy, but there was something so inviting about their fire, the easy laughter and the smell of food roasting that made me stay a moment longer. The two men stood near the fire and were singing some folk tale by the sound of it. The woman sat on the step of the caravan, looking as though she was re-painting or finishing off a bowl ready to be sold. A younger girl sat at the fire on a thick log, a fiddle in her hands and tucked to her shoulder, and a boy half my age was turning a spit with what looked like a lamb roast from a sheep that would not have belonged to these travelers. A small family, I thought, looking for a quiet place to stay perhaps.

The woman looked up suddenly, her eyes and ears quicker in the night than I had given her credit for. She stood. "Hey, show yourself!"

The men stopped their singing and the fiddle stilled. All turned quickly, warily, to where I stood in the shadows. I recognized their apprehension and felt a sort of kindred spirit to them. Outsiders. Unwanted. That was how I felt.

I stepped from the shadows of the trees. "I'm on my own. My name's Seb. I saw your fire."

"And smelled our meat, no doubt in it," the woman said, pointing her fine paintbrush in my direction. I stammered an apology. She gave a sudden grin. "We'll not begrudge a boy something to eat on a cold night. Come and warm your bones, lad." She pointed to the fire.

I came forward, and the bigger of the two men—a man with black hair and a long, drooping mustache, clapped a hand on my shoulder. "Too cold watching the flocks is it?"

I realized that in my current garb, they wouldn't recognize me as a cadet Dragon Rider. I was about to say something, but he gave a laugh, clapping me on the shoulder again and guiding me to a warm spot near the fire.

"Never mind, lad, we won't tell if you won't. I've spent a lot of nights standing on hillsides, hoping I don't get chased by wolves or eaten by bears! Roluz, cut a slice of meat for our new friend!"

The boy—Roluz by the name of him—stuck his tongue out me, but did as his father bade.

The man waved a hand. "I am Arkady, and this is my family. My daughter Afiyah, my son Roluz, my brother Turri, and my beautiful wife Sansha." He wheeled his big arms in the air again, encompassing his whole family and most of the night. "We are from Shaar, a land far, far to the west and far, far to the south."

"What are you doing so near Torvald?" I asked, feeling the warmth already creeping into my feet and grateful for it. The meat was good, hot in my fingers and tasty. I wolfed it down as if I'd had no meal in days.

"Ha, you northerners! Very blunt. I like it!" Arkady slapped his knee. "Your dragons bring us here, of course. Everywhere we go, we are told about the Dragon Riders of the mountain-city, and I swore that before I got too old I would take my family to see them." He leaned closer. "It is also a good time to be near to dragons—for the stories we have heard tell of trouble brewing."

I frowned at those words, but Arkady's brother swatted him with a brightly coloured handkerchief. "You see trouble in every shadow. It might have been better if you had waited for summer, no?"

"No," Arkady said. He shook his head and smoothed his mustache.

"Don't scare the boy." Sansha looked up from the bowl she had painted. She put it down and came to the fire. "There's enough trouble in the world without bringing it to our door by speaking of it."

Arkady shook his head. "Oh, trouble comes if we talk of it or not." He pulled a pipe from a pocket inside his vest and began to tap down tobacco into the white bowl of the pipe. Leaning down, he pulled a split of wood from the fire. When he had smoke curling from his pipe, he turned to me. "Do you want to hear a story? A story they probably have not told you, living behind those high walls of your city?"

"Arkady Bismollah Shaar," Sansha said. She tugged a black woolen shawl closer about her. "Do not scare the lad."

"And what of his right to know the truth—of the old troubles stirring?" Arkady sounded defiant, and I couldn't help but wonder if his story would end with his hand out so he might lift whatever curse might stain my life. The gypsies were known to both be light of hand and light of tongue, but I was curious now. The men in town had talked of war brewing—of trouble. And now this gypsy was saying the same. Did he know of something that had gone unnoticed by Dragon Rider patrols?

"Tell me, please," I asked. Sansha shook her head and stood.

"Come Afiyah and Roluz. Your bed calls for you two."

Roluz put up a fuss and dragged his heels, but Afiyah took her fiddle with her and followed her mother to the caravan.

I looked from Arkady to Turri. "What tales do you hear?"

The two men swapped a look that left me uneasy—there was real fear in these men's eyes, and gypsies did not scare easily.

Turri put another log on the fire so it flamed up high, and Arkady leaned close. "The tales of Dragon Riders flying over the skies, ah, we all hear these. Why, in past times, it's said so many dragons took to the air that the skies turned black with their wings, and even the coldest night was warmed with their fiery breath. But these were the old days, when Torvald was but a small town, and riders it is said had barely learned to live with dragons. In those times, whole mountain ranges were torn apart by their epic fights, and some of the largest dragons were almost the size of the city itself beneath us."

I leaned forward and wondered how much of this could be true. I'd never heard the tales of old—my father didn't hold with stories, and so I'd only caught snatches of the old stories, overheard from other boys.

Arkady puffed on his pipe and stared into the fire as if seeing the olden times. "They fought each other, these riders and dragons of old. And they fought different tribes, but then a greater evil rose." He looked at Turri, who stood with his arms tight across his chest, and then Arkady looked at me. He leaned closer and his voice dropped low. "It was then that the Darkening rose."

I sat with my mouth open as I heard bits and pieces about some old enemy—the Darkening. I whispered the word, and Arkady nodded. "Do you know why it's was called that? It was because it was like forgetfulness…a black stain that spread across the land. People vanished or disappeared inside darkness that came over them, never to be seen again. Realms started to shrink. The people forgot the paths to their villages, and even forgot the people they loved…their homes seemed more like something remembered in a dream than a real place that was lost. It was like there was a power slowly stealing the world, one village at a time."

My frown tightened. "How do you know this if everyone forgets?"

Turri gave a snort, but Arkady puffed on his pipe and nodded. "A good question—and one that can be answered in the story. For while the Darkening was a power that brought grave evil, it was pushed back and defeated."

"How?" I breathed out the word, feeling how cold the dark night really was beyond the fire.

Arkady smiled. "With dragon fire—and magic. The Darkening bonded the riders together, made them one force. That and the magical jewels they found. It was only the wisest of the Dragon Riders who knew of these precious stones—rare, special jewels shaped like a dragon's egg that they learned of from their dragons. With fire and magic, the riders drove back the Darkening. But it took many years and many lives. For it took the riders years of following clues and riddles and rumors until riders found them all. When the riders returned, riding on their dragons with those magical jewels, well—there was hardly any kingdom left. People couldn't remember who the king was or where the roads led to." Arkady pulled on his pipe, but it had gone out. He tapped it against his palm. "The dragons and their stones overcame the Darkening."

"Or not," Turri mumbled darkly. Arkady shot him a look.

"What do you mean?" I asked Turri, but he shied his glance away.

Arkady sighed heavily. He glanced behind him as if worried, and then looked at me again. "There are roadside tales and passed-down gossip starting up again that in the far north, people are forgetting things once again. Village names, where this mountain stood, where that field lies. Some say the Darkening never really left, but was biding its time for a return…that it has come back. And many wonder if the Dragon Riders will be able to defeat it again."

Turri gave another snort. "The dragons are fat and lazy, the riders a bunch of children—and the magic is lost. We live in dark days, boy. I'm not sure we're safe even near the dragons."

I shifted on the log. All this talk of magical stones was starting to make this seem like a tale for children. Still, the stories made me think of what I had heard in the city as well. I asked Arkady, "That is why you are here? To be near the dragons—just in case they can hold back this…the Darkening?"

Arkady put away his pipe and straightened. "We are here to see the dragons." He gave a firm nod, but I saw a look slip between Arkady and Turri. I thought that while the city folk welcomed the gypsies as travelers, they might not welcome them to stay on longer than a short stay. Arkady seemed to see what I was thinking, for he forced a smile. "The people of the Shaar are brave, but we do not belong on battlefields…or in cites. We belong on the free roads. We will go on as we have, trading, making things, always moving."

I looked from him to Turri and back. "What if you forget the roads, too? What if you forget your people?"

Arkady and Turri swapped another look, and Turri shook his head. "Let's talk of better things. When do you think the first snow will come to the mountains, brother?"

The two men began to talk of weather, of the seasons changing. I sat, staring into the fire.

First the rumors of war, and now this talk of the return of the Darkening. I shifted uneasy on the log, no longer warmed by the fire. Perhaps these were just travelers' tales—but perhaps something was stirring. But why hadn't the Dragon Rider patrols come back with news of this?

And then I thought about the forgetting—what if the patrols forgot what they had seen? Or what if…what if the Darkening moved in utter darkness, slipping past in such blackness that not even a dragon could see it. I shivered.

I stayed for a little while longer. Turri fell silent, brooding over the talk, I thought. And Arkady took up another story of their travels from the south. But I knew I had to get back to the academy. The moon rose and I stood to make my goodbyes.

Before I left, I told him, "Tomorrow, if you want to see dragons, go over to the mountain lake. Everyone knows the dragons often fish that lake—Hammal Lake it's called."

Arkady clapped a hand on my shoulder. "Farewell, shepherd boy. Do not let the dark frighten you."

I nodded. But it was not darkness that worried me—it was old enemies of the dragons and the thought that they might be coming back.

CHAPTER 15

VOICES IN THE NIGHT

A soft tapping drifted into my dreams of flying with Kalax, the wind in my face and Seb grinning at me. I blinked my eyes, waking to see I was alone in the tiny cold room that had been allotted to me on my first day here. Varla had gone home for a few days to visit her sick mother. Our room was in the main stone keep of the academy. Unlike my room at home, which had thick tapestries and rugs, this room had two beds, a wooden table with a lamp, wooden trunks to hold our clothes, and nothing more. It was cold, drafty and sometimes the kestrels swooped and called outside my window.

The room was high in the keep, which made it surprising to realize someone was actually tapping on the glass of that window. Getting up, I pulled a blanket over my shoulders and stumbled to the window. The cold of the stone chilled my bare feet. A face loomed against the misted glass. I peered out at shaggy brown hair and pale features.

"Seb?" Unlatching the window let in a gust of cold night air. I pulled my blanket tighter. "What do you think you are doing?" The cold left me shivering, but I helped Seb to climb over the sill. He dropped onto the floor, panting, but looking a lot warmer in his woolen cloak. "You could have been killed," I told him.

Seb threw back his cloak. He had on his old clothes, not the cadet uniform, and he smelled of wood smoke. "What have you been doing? Did you sneak out of the academy?"

Brushing at the leaves and twigs stuck to his breeches, he grinned. "It's not so bad out there, there's ivy up this whole side of the keep, and the oak's got strong limbs you can climb to get started. But I had to speak to you. I heard something important."

"It couldn't wait until morning?" Shivering, I pulled my blanket tighter again and shifted from one foot to the other. "And what could you have heard? Something from your dreams?" I was skeptical. Not only did Sebastian seem intent on ruining our ranking in class, it also seemed like he was dead set on breaking every rule and getting us thrown out of the academy altogether.

"I went out to clear my head."

I sighed, went back to my bed and sat on the edge. I wanted to put my head in my hands and howl. Instead, I turned and picked up the striking flint to light the lamp on the table. When it glowed a soft yellow, I turned to Seb. "What am I going to do? You're a criminal. You are a career criminal!"

"No, I just needed to get away. You're lucky to have a room to yourself. I don't. Anyway, that's not the point. The point is...something bad is stirring. I've heard about it twice now."

I stared at him. "What are you talking about? The Dragon

Riders are on regular patrols. They haven't come back to report anything. There are no armies gathering. We're at peace with all the other realms." I peered closer at him. "Are you drunk?"

He came closer. "Have you heard of the Darkening?" he said earnestly.

I had to roll my eyes, but I couldn't stop another shiver, too. I forced a gruff tone into my voice—I didn't want to think about those old stories, not in the middle of night. "Of course. Every child hears those old legends. People falling sick, struck dumb, disappearing entirely. But that's...it's all just old fairy tales."

"No," Seb said in a half-whisper. "No, it isn't." He sat down on the bed next to me and took a deep breath. "When I went out the other night, down to the city, I heard two men talking about war, about trouble brewing in the north."

"People always talk." I waved my hand as if I could swat away his words. "The riders on patrol haven't reported anything."

"Well, what if that's because they can't see it from the air? What if it's hidden in darkness? Besides, when you hear something in Monger's Lane, you listen. Trust me, I know about that. Sure, folks will gossip and argue—but in Monger's Lane rumors are always about others. If the men there are worried about war it's because that's a threat to them. Besides, I heard the same story from travelers again tonight. Hearing the same thing twice is not good."

"Okay, that kind of makes sense," I said, begrudging him the idea he might be right.

Seb nodded. "The travelers came here to be safe near the dragons, but they're worried that not even the dragons will be able to turn back this…this Darkening. They say even in the south they hear tales coming back from the far north, and that others are fleeing the edges of the realm." Seb's face was pale in the weak lamplight. "It can't be a coincidence that these stories are spreading."

I shook my head. "It still doesn't make sense. There's been twenty years of absolute peace, and hundreds of years of only small battles before that. Who would dare come against the Dragon Riders? Besides, why hasn't anyone else heard about this? Why are you the only one seeing this?" I rubbed by eyes and forehead. My head had starting to thud.

"I keep telling you—the Darkening makes people forget. What if patrols saw something—and then forgot. We're hearing stories right now from travelers and poor woodsmen, Thea, and you're a friend of the prince. All the noble families know each other. You can ask him about this."

I lifted my eyebrows high. "And what am I supposed to ask him? Excuse me, Prince Justin, have you heard the old fairy tales about the Darkening? And is it coming back for us?" I felt my cheeks starting to burn just at the mere thought of it. "He would laugh at me and think that I was being a panicky little girl who didn't know enough to tell a children's story from fact. You really are trying to get us kicked out, aren't you?"

"So you'd rather do nothing?" His eyes went wide.

I pushed out a long breath. "Well, if people are talking, I guess I could tell the prince that— it would show I am at least in touch with the people, and he ought to know. So…okay. This once, I'll do it."

"Yes, I knew you would!" Seb punched the air, his enthusiasm echoing around the chamber.

"Shhh!" I hushed him, holding a hand up. In the distance, a door slammed and I heard the slap of shoes on cold stone.

A knock sounded on my door, and then a woman's harsh voice rose up. "Agathea? Are you awake?"

Matron. I mouthed the word at Seb and put a finger to my lips to keep him quiet.

The maid and matron of these quarters was an older woman who supervised the cleaning of the keep. Normally, the matron would only need to oversee academy staff, but with two female cadets she had been given added responsibility over us and she made it clear she didn't like that one bit. She treated me as if I was a stone around her neck, and I knew she'd be just as happy to see me thrown out. Finding Seb in my room was a violation of the rules, and that would be the second mark against me and Seb.

I called out, "Yes, Matron—I was just dreaming. Sorry if I woke you."

"Get back to sleep. You'll wake the whole keep with dreams like that!" she spoke harshly, but I heard her retreating steps.

I felt bad about the lie. I had never lied to anyone—not my father or my mother or my brothers, but since meeting Seb my life had become more than complicated. I turned to face him.

He gave me a grin. "Quick thinking."

Getting up, I went to the window. "You have to go. Now. You can't be caught in my room. I'll see if I can speak to Prince Justin tomorrow. And don't get caught climbing down from here."

Seb nodded. He strode to the window, climbed back out and clung to the ivy that wound up the stone. With a final grin, he disappeared from view.

I closed the window, but stood next to it, staring out at the night, hoping Seb would make it back to the ground safely. By the First Dragon, what was he getting me into? Him and his stories, I thought. I bit my lower lip and wondered if Sebastian even knew how dangerous the things he was doing could be? He could get himself hurt, and us both thrown out of the academy, and then our days of dragon riding would be over.

But what if the stories he had heard were true?

I shivered, but I couldn't go back to bed. The night was cold enough to mist the window again, and I couldn't see the stars in the darkness. The Darkening—it is just a tale, I thought. But what if it was more? I wished then that my mother had let my father tell me more—or that my brothers had told me more of the stories. But I remembered the dream I'd had—that nightmare of feeling like I had been swallowed by darkness, that I had felt the life and heat draining from my body.

"Just a dream," I muttered to myself, and I headed to my bed. Under the covers, the down-feather mattress sinking to hold me, I shivered. By Kalax's hot breath, how was I to convey to the prince these stories without sounding like a child myself? I lay there awake for a very long time, thinking of that.

But I was also thinking of battle—of the chance to do more than prove myself a Dragon Rider on long patrols. What if there was danger coming? Would I get the chance to show not just my father but everyone that I was someone as worthy as the Dragon Riders in the sagas of old?

CHAPTER 16

MOUNTAIN STORIES

Morning came too early for me. Seb and his stories had kept me awake, and so I rose with heavy eyes and dragging feet. We were expected to continue with our flying practice, I had to once again promise Seb that I would endeavor to see the prince.

But first I had only one thing I wanted to think about— flying Kalax!

I'd been working with Seb to try and feel the dragon's thoughts. It pushed away any fear—but it wasn't so much the flying that strung my nerves tight, it was the fear of falling. Putting my focus on Kalax made it better, and I'd gotten so I hardly worried about jumping up into the saddle. Today, the cadets were all practicing the skills we had learned during our weeks of training on the ground and on our fake dragons. This time, however, we would be mounted on real dragons as we glided, swooped and soared.

For me, this meant unslinging my bow and trying to hit tall targets that had been fixed onto the end of the dragon platforms on top of the walls. We were to choose moments when we would have a clear shot across the dragon's back or neck without the dragon's wings in the way. Our arrows were blunted, so that no stray shot would hurt any dragon. The tips were also daubed with paint, so any hit—stray or accurate—would be marked. Any cadets who shot their own dragon would be in for a stern lecture from the instructors, and a lot of ribbing from the other cadets.

To start with, it was more than awkward. My arrows kept getting caught in strong gusts from Kalax's vast leathery wings. But the connection with Kalax that Seb was teaching me made it easier. I could feel the heartbeat of the animal reverberating underneath and through me—it matched the beat of her wings, and I tried to match my breaths and slow my too-quick pulse to match hers.

I hit the target once out of five fly-overs, which was the best that any of us trainees did. And I didn't hit Kalax—not once. Beris, on his big blue dragon, managed to scrape the poor beast's wing with one of his practice arrows, causing his dragon to flinch and dive, almost throwing both its riders off of its back.

By mid-afternoon we were all saddle-sore and weary. My arms ached from the effort of holding the bow drawn for the long moments it took to get a clear shot—I wanted to be able to shoot like I did on land, with fast pulls and releases. How am I ever going to get the hang of this? I thought.

As Kalax landed, Seb made his usual cooing sounds at the beast to soothe her. I just stowed my bow and arrow with the ties meant to hold them to my saddle. On a sudden impulse, I leaned down to put my hands on her warm scaly side, wishing her thanks for keeping me alive for the past few hours.

There was a pleased rumble from deep inside the dragon. She was purring. "I didn't know that dragons purred," I said and unclipped my harness.

"Kalax does, but I haven't heard Jensen's or Beris' dragons doing so yet," Seb said. He nodded over to the top of the stone wall. "Look over there—the prince. Now's your chance."

"Okay, okay." I shushed him with my hands, feeling ugly and unready. I was sweaty, stinky and dirty from flying, and the prince looked, well, like he always did—perfect in his Dragon Rider's uniform of a leather jerkin with the badge of a rider, his leather breeches and high boots.

The prince stood near our target with Ryan and one of the other instructors. The choice about talking to him was taken out of my hands as the prince looked up, saw me and beckoned me over. I gulped. No time to change or even wash my face, which I knew had to be stained from dirt and sweat.

"Go on," Seb said, nudging me with an elbow. Kalax chirruped and lifted her head. Seb bend over to dismantle the harness from her shoulders and around her wings.

I trudged over to the end of the platform.

Ryan grinned at me. "Cadet, you're not looking so terrified up there now."

Hearing the teasing in his voice, I shot him a murderous look but mumbled a thanks. Ryan grinned and gestured to the instructor that he was ready to move on. "Let's check the other targets for any near hits. Do you think they need more time on their fake dragons to improve their aim?" The two walked off, talking training techniques and bemoaning the current crop of cadets.

Prince Justin turned to me. "Actually, I thought you did very well, even hitting the target."

Face hot, I forced a smile. "If I only hit one enemy out of every five, the city is going to be in a bad state by the end of any battle." I noticed Justin's jaw tighten just a tad. Oops. Obviously the wrong joke to make.

But he relaxed and a faint smile appeared. "It took me a good week before I could hit anything. The fact that you hit the target and you didn't score a hole through your dragon's wing on your very first day is impressive. It seems that you are doing well." He looked behind me, to where Sebastian was spending more time scratching Kalax than he was wrestling with the harness. "How is your partner? Before, you had some worries about him?"

Now my face burned for having even mentioned that to my prince. "Oh, he's... a good navigator, actually, very in tune with the dragon. I just...well, I think it's just that he's a terrible student…I think." I shrugged and let the rest of the words trail off.

Prince Justin chuckled.

Deciding to drop the formality, and talk to him how I had used to talk to him back when we were both children, I said, "There was something that I wanted to ask you about, actually."

"Anything."

I wouldn't get into the habit of promising anything, my prince! I thought.

He gestured to the stairs. "Will you walk with me?"

I went ahead of him, heading down to the training area and the keep. Inside the keep, in the great room, the staff always put out pitchers of wine and water, and set out a table with cheese and bread for training days. We'd all learned to eat light during the day, and hearty only at the end of the day—you never wanted to go up on a dragon with a full stomach. Jensen had done that once, and had lost his breakfast onto his dragon—his navigator, Wil, wouldn't speak to him for three days after that, and his dragon wouldn't let Jenson mount if Jenson so much as had a whiff of bacon on his breath.

The prince poured out a goblet of water for me and I took it. My throat was suddenly dry and my stomach kept jumping. "The students have been hearing rumors of late."

"Rumors?" he asked, arching an eyebrow. He poured wine into one of the pewter goblets in use at the academy.

I shrugged and waved vaguely to the north. "I know, perhaps just talk, but we've been hearing stories coming out of the north, out of the mountains. Of trouble brewing. Something the patrols may not be seeing."

He gestured to the bench set near the table. I shook my head. I didn't want to sit down. With a nod, he asked, "What stories exactly?"

"Oh, just...trouble. Villages in need, people starting to move south out of harm's way, that maybe there would even be a need for the Dragon Riders..." My words faded off. He had tipped his head to one side, and I couldn't tell if he was thinking that I was being foolish or not.

The prince paused for a fraction. He wet his lips and shook his head. "Really, there is nothing to worry about. I attend the king's council meetings every day and hear the reports from every patrol that comes in. The realm is secure."

"Oh, I'm sure, if you suggest there is nothing to worry about, then of course there isn't. But...well, talk can be trouble, too. Where do you think these rumors come from?"

Prince Justin sipped his wine and shrugged. "Where else? The mountains and the north breed trouble and fear and nightmares.

They always have. And if it is not merchants talking to raise the price of their goods, it is gypsies spreading tales to pull a few coins into their hands or to make excuses why they need to stay on and not head to the dry south so soon, or it is lazy workers seeking a reason to stay home by the fire. Or it is simply talk spread so that folks might puff up their own importance that they know more than anyone else. Honestly, if the Dragon Riders were to follow every tale brought to the king's council we would be in the skies every day and night. Now, drink up and smile," he said, raising his goblet. "Cheers."

I gulped down the water and decided to see just how far I could press my luck. "But what if there is more to the talk this time? If your people are worried, should we not at least make efforts to calm everyone? Perhaps double patrols? And is there anything…anything…I should be preparing for, as someone who will one day be a Dragon Rider?"

His smile softened. "My dear, you really don't have to worry about anything. You know that I would never see you come to harm or thrown into harm's way."

A flash of annoyance sizzled through me. How dare he mollycoddle me, as if I was a weak woman who needed a man to hold my sword. I was training to be not just a rider, but a protector. Chin high, I stared at him and said through gritted teeth, "I aim to defend my city, my realm, my king and my prince with all my strength, sire." I straightened. I wore the uniform of a

153

cadet—and the badge of the academy.

He seemed to realize that he had offended me, for he swept a bow. "I mean no disrespect, and I had rather wished that I didn't have to say this, but let me make clear my meaning. I know you and your family, Thea. I fly with your brother, and your eldest brother is captain of my squadrons, but I do not want to worry your father for his only daughter. To that end, I will do all to ensure you are kept safe."

"Thank you. Your consideration for my family is warmly received, but please do remember, the Flammas have protected Torvald for generations. And my father would be proud of any service I could render."

The prince nodded. He glanced around us as if looking for who might overhear, and then he dropped his voice lower. "I will confide in you, Thea. There are rumors—stories have reached the king's council. We hear more than most think we do. However, for the most part, it seems the usual winter scare stories. The council is not eager to act rashly—if we give validity to these tales, we may start a panic that is unnecessary. But, please, you have my word, we do worry, and we are beginning to wonder."

I gripped my goblet more tightly. "What do you think is happening?"

Justin shook his head. "No one can really say for sure. I suspect we may be seeing restlessness in some of the mountain villages—border folk, not Torvald citizens—have had hard winters these last few years. There might not be anything wrong at all, more than the deep snows have convinced them to move south, or they've been hit by some sickness. As yet, the king sees no reason for alarm."

Or maybe the Darkening is returning. I didn't say it, but I frowned in thought.

"But enough of such talk!" He smiled and lifted his goblet again. "We should toast to your first armed flight. May the rest of your training go just as well!"

I lifted my goblet and clinked it against his, but I was left wondering if I needed to learn everything I need to know as fast as I could before I had to use it in a real battle.

*   *   *

"Okay, tonight it is then," I said, rounding on Seb.

"What?" He stared at me, his forehead, eyes and mouth knotted with confusion. I had managed to track him down to the equipment sheds where he was busy polishing the dragon saddles and harnesses, inspecting all the tack we used on Kalax. I realized I had never even considered this part of my duty as a Dragon Rider, and it was obvious that neither did Beris or Jensen, the other cadet protectors. Somehow, I just thought that Kalax's harness should always be gleaming and fit beautifully, but I hadn't given any thought to making certain that it did.

I imagined, somehow, that just like my father's horses, there must be stable boys who cared for the dragon saddles. I thought they would look after both the Dragon Riders and the cadet's equipment. Now I saw that, for Kalax at least, Seb was doing the upkeep.

It must be his smithy background, I thought. The harness links shone and were perfectly fitted for an easy and strong connection. The leather had been polished. I was impressed at Seb's devotion to our red, and I wondered if all of the navigators were like this. I didn't think they were. I had overlooked this part of what he did for us—our lives depended on the buckles and leather being strong and holding. Seb might have been weak in training—and might ignore a lot of rules—but a growing respect for him stirred inside my chest. Seb had his priorities right. I wanted to make sure mine were in order, too.

"Tonight you're going to take me to see these gypsies of yours," I said. I told him what I heard from the prince. Spreading my hands wide, I told him, "He just about admitted me that there is something weird going on in the mountains to the north. We need to know more, and I don't think I'm going to get anything more from him."

"The Darkening." Seb muttered the word. His eyes went wide, in equal parts fear and excitement, I guessed. I was feeling about the same right now.

"And he just said all this to you?" Seb asked. He turned to make sure that the saddles were securely sitting on the hooks that held them to the stone wall.

I crossed my arms. "What—you don't believe me? Look, if something is going on, we should be ready. I want you to take me to see your gypsy friends, and I want to know everything that I can learn about the Darkening."

He glanced at me sideways. "I thought you knew all those old children's stories?"

I pressed my lips tight so I wouldn't bite off his head. I didn't want to admit that I knew way too little. I was also not going to go and ask my brothers. They'd only make fun of me, and Mother had made it clear that if they ever told me those stories and she found out—well, my brothers were far more terrified of Mother than they ever had been of Father. And asking any of the other cadets or instructors was out too—I did not want to look a fool in front of any of them.

Pulling in a breath, I let it out and said, "Seb—focus. We need to go see the travelers."

He leaned against the saddle and the corner of his mouth lifted. "But, you know, isn't that breaking the rules? I thought you wanted to be the perfect cadet? Top of your class? Best ever?"

I hated that he was throwing my words at me—and that, yes, I still wanted that. Letting my arms fall to my side, I asked him, "What's more important—the rules or learning what we need to know to survive? If...and that's a big if...the Darkening, or whatever that is, has come back, and we know less than most children know, then we're not going to be able to fight it. That means we're going to be the first ones dead. And Kalax, too."

I saw Seb's throat work. He straightened. I hated to hit him where it hurt most—I knew how much he cared for our dragon, how close a bond he had formed. Much more than the one I had made. But I also knew I was right. The only place we were going to find out what we needed to know was with the gypsies.

"Tonight," I repeated, making my voice firm. "We'll go in the hours after dinner and before bedtime like we're out for a training run. Everyone expects me to put in extra runs, and I'll drag you with me. And it's not breaking the rules if we're back early enough."

Seb looked like he wanted to protest—I could see the doubt in his eyes—but I was having none of it. I walked away, giving him no opportunity to back out of my plan. We were going to talk to the gypsies and I was going to hear these stories for myself. And then we could figure out how to train so we could be ready.

CHAPTER 17

BACK TO THE CAMP

Waiting for Thea was never fun. I paced nervously by the side of an equipment shed, making sure to stay in the shadows and making no sound. Already I had seen four Dragon Riders walk past me on their way to the kitchens for food and wine. From the keep, I could hear the noise of singing and loud talk as cadets and riders had gathered to sit in front of the fire in the great hearth or to play cards or swap stories or just to sit and doze or eat a good meal.

The last few hours of the night were officially leisure hours for everyone, except the most essential staff within the academy. Many of the Dragon Riders would come by to spend time with the cadets, and the instructors sometimes stopped by to share a word of wisdom or comment on how the day's training had gone. It was usually a time I looked forward to, but some cadets looked down on it, preferring to go into town for an hour or two. I knew we wouldn't be missed if we didn't show our faces.

I gathered my old woolen cloak closer. I'd dressed again in my old clothes, and I wondered if Thea would as well, or if she would wear her cadet uniform. That might spook the gypsies, but then again, maybe they would be impressed to meet a real soon-to-be Dragon Rider. I didn't know. Luckily, it was a warm evening. The sky had gone a dusky purple and the moon was rising early, a sliver of silver above the walls and the trees just now. I had packed a small knapsack of things we might need— baked goods taken from the kitchen to share with the gypsies, a striking flint, just in case we needed light, and an extra, oil-treated blanket in case it rained.

"Psst!"

I jumped at the hissing sound and turned to see someone who looked like a scullery maid walking toward me. But Thea's golden hair, glinting in the torchlight from the keep, gave her away. She had dressed in a large, unkempt cloak, skirts and a blouse. I was going to guess she had borrowed these from one of the staff. She had even gone so far as to mess up her hair and smudge a bit of ash on her face as if she'd gotten dirty from sweeping out the fireplaces.

"What happened to you looking like you were going out for a run?" I asked.

"Come on," she hissed, not stopping as she passed me. I caught up with her as she was striding purposefully out of the front gate.

The guards on duty saw us and nodded, saying nothing. We must look like a pair of academy staff returning home for the night. A sudden thrill of freedom chased down my spine. The academy always felt to me like everyone was watching me, judging me. Now, outside on the mountain, I could breathe in and not worry what anyone thought. The air cooled. The wind rose with no barrier of a wall to hold it back.

I kept pace with Thea until we had rounded the first turn in the lane. Grabbing her cloak, I pulled her behind the boulder and onto the goat path that led up and away over the ridge.

"You never told me we were climbing up there," Thea said, her voice low. "I would have picked warmer clothes."

"Arkady and his people were camping up here, but I told him to head to Hammal Lake to see the dragons fly, so they might have moved there." After our flying lessons ended, the dragons were released and allowed to swoop and dive down over the cold surfaces of the water, seizing the salmon and other fish that spawned in the lake in huge numbers. I hoped the gypsies had seen the dragons fishing, like gigantic sea eagles, and had stayed to camp at the lake. The travelers might be fishing there, too.

Thea grumbled about the climb, but I could tell she didn't mean it. Unlike me, she never ran out of breath. We climbed until my thighs started to burn. Cresting the ridge that ran behind the academy, I paused for a moment and turned. Beyond the enclosure where the dragons lived and the towers and walls of the academy, the city spread in circles of firelight. The dark shadows of evening spreading over the valleys, leaving the farms in darkness and the peaks and tops of trees picked out in light. It was like looking at one of the aerial maps.

I heard Thea's sigh, and glanced over. She was looking up at the sky and the stars now popping out like a river of light. The air was so clear and cold that each star glittered as bright as sparks from the hottest forge, sparkling and glinting.

After a moment of wonder, the cold roused me. I bumped Thea's arm and we went down the other side of the mountain, our steps quick now to keep warm. We crossed into the scrubby woodlands and high meadows of the wilder, northern side of the mountain.

It wasn't long before we saw the sheen of Hammal Lake, ringed by the black trees. The smell of roasting fish and mutton carried to us on the night breeze along with a faint tune played on a whistle and followed by a fiddle. The song seemed a sad, lonely one.

Both mine and Thea's stomachs grumbled, and we shared a quick look. Thea grimaced. I shrugged. The walk had made us both hungry. We crossed down to the woods, and followed the smell of cooking to a small, sandy shore along one of the coves at the lake's edge.

"Ho, Arkady! Sansha," I called out. I could see the glimmer of a campfire through the trees now.

"Seb! Our wandering herdsman." Arkady laughed and sprang

up. "I hope you have not come to collect a missing sheep. You see, this one was very old and near the end of its prime anyway." He grinned and nodded at his brother Turri.

"No, Arkady, not looking for any stray lambs. I'm just here to share your fire and repay you for your kindness of the night." I stepped out of the shadows. Arkady and Turri stood by the fire as they had the other night. This time, Sansha tending to the spit and roast, and to a pan of fish. Afiyah once again sat on a large log near the fire and had her fiddle out and Roluz lowered a small, penny whistle.

I pulled the baked goods—sourbread and oat muffins—from my knapsack. Sansha, her eyebrows lifted high and her dark eyes bright in the firelight, rose to take them and asked, "Who is this? You didn't tell us you had a sweetheart?" Sansha waved Thea to the fire.

"Oh, we're not…" I started to stumble over the words, thankful for the shadows so that they would not see my face flame.

Thea shot me a hard stare and said, "My name is Thea. I'm his…sister."

I almost choked. Thea looked nothing like me. Her hair was golden and fine. My dark and always stuck up. She was finely made, with small hands. My hands and feet always seemed too big for me.

163

Arkady looked from one of us to the other and shook his head. "Ah, never mind, never mind. The more the merrier, I say. And today we saw the most spectacular sight. Dragons as large as three, four, five caravans swooping and skimming the surface of the lake, seizing fish as if they were tidbits and flying off." He mimed the movement, flapping and swooping his arms.

"And then, after they had their fill, they would land in the lake and roll over, cleaning their wings and paddle through the water as if they were swans." He let out a breath. "Ah, it was such a sight. But come…let us eat first, and then we'll have stories to share."

Afiyah and Roluz put away the fiddle and the whistle. Again, there were no plates. Sansha cooled the pan and then it was passed around, and fish taken from the pan with fingers. Bread was passed. Turri and Arkady cut off hunks of meat from the roast and these were passed around as well.

After the feast, Arkady leaned back and patted his stomach. "Really, I have to thank you for being so welcoming, shepherd of Mount Hammal. I never thought I would get to show my children the dragons. If there is anything that the people of Shaar can do for you, then tell us now."

Thea sat up. "Actually, sir, apart from your excellent company and music, we came to hear—I came so I might hear your stories."

"Anything, child," Arkady said.

"The Darkening," she said. "I want you to tell me more about the Darkening. What is it? Where is it?"

Arkady frowned. He pulled on his long moustaches. "And your brother can't tell you? This is grave talk for such a merry night."

"But we need to know. I want to hear this for myself," Thea said and spread her hands wide.

Arkady glanced at me. "You have a sister who has her own mind, eh?"

I spread my hands and muttered, "You have no idea."

He looked to Turri and then Sansha. Turri shrugged and walked way, muttering, "I will water the horse."

Sansha rose as well and took the pan with her, telling the children to come along for a wash in the lake.

Arkady sat down next to me on the log and looked from me to Thea. "Fine. I will tell you what stories and tales I have already told your…told to Seb, though that is not a lot," he warned.

Sitting forward, elbows on her knees, Thea nodded.

He told the same story he'd told me of the Darkening. "Some call it a sickness, and some an army of darkness. It has not been seen for the last hundred years, but the old tales were always of how it made villages disappear and people forget. Some legends even say the Darkening is caused by a magic, that a stone the size of your fist and the colour of grass can make men's mind go blank and women lose the memory of even their own children's names. Others say the Darkening is the fault of a wizard who tried to take over the world with his spells."

Thea was frowning and opened her mouth as if she might say something insulting. I jumped in before she could. "And the Dragon Riders can beat this—right?"

"So the stories say. In all the tales, only the Dragon Riders with their fire and might could burn out the Darkening and restore the people's memory. They could turn the magic to good uses."

Thea glanced at me and rolled her eyes. I knew what she was thinking. This sounded like a fairy tale to me, too. How could a dragon burn someone and give them their memory back? Getting caught by dragon fire would kill anyone.

Arkady pulled out his pipe, but he did not put tobacco in it or light it. "One tale my grandmother told me said that the Darkening came with an evil army of black dragons, and that it was the battle between black dragons and Dragon Riders which drove off this terrible thing." He shrugged. "I do not know. But in all the tales, there is always a battle, and fire, and lots of people are hurt."

Thea nudged me and stood. "Thank you. We wish you luck on

your travels."

It seemed rude to me to hurry off, but I had no choice other than to say goodnight and leave with her. I hurried to catch up with her and then walked next to her in silence. I didn't know if she believed the stories—I still wasn't sure I did. I was only certain that Thea, just like I, was as caught up in thoughts of darkness, war and fire.

*   *   *

The moon had set by the time we crept back into the academy. The gates stood open, but we had to wait for a moment when the guards had walked across the gap and turned to look out past the walls before we could slip across the walls. We crossed the open training area, heading for the kitchens. The staff would be asleep, and we could sneak in the back. Inside the kitchen, I pulled off my cloak.

Thea put her hand on my arm. "Thank you. For tonight, I mean. For taking me to hear the stories myself."

I shrugged. "I'm not sure what good they are. I mean, if Dragon Riders had magical stones, why don't they have them still? Why don't we know about them?"

She frowned and shook her head.

A sudden square of light fell over us. We looked to the doorway to see Mordecai standing there, a lantern above his head.

In the dim light, he looked even grimmer and meaner than usual. His hair lank about his face, his shoulders hunched, and two angry spots of colour high on his cheeks. He pulled a cloak tighter around his shoulders. "By the First Dragon, what—are you stealing food?"

We both froze. There was nothing we could do now we'd been seen. I waited, tense and nervous, as he came into the kitchen. Was it worse to be sneaking in or to be thought to be stealing food?

He pushed the door open wide and stepped forward, peering at us. "What are you doing, sneaking around like a thief? This is your second mark against you, isn't it, cadet? One more and you're out of the academy. But perhaps you should be charged with two marks? Both for thieving and sneaking."

I lifted my chin. "I'm not a thief. I've never taken anything that wasn't given to me."

His lip curled. "But you don't deny the sneaking, do you. How dare you think the rules do not apply to you? As for you…" He turned and jabbed a finger at Thea. "I'd thought better of you, Cadet Flamma. Your brother Ryan was a bit of a handful in his time, but I thought you had the dash of Reynalt about you. Serious, dedicated. I see you're just as willful as your partner. Doesn't seem to matter to either of you to put your minds to learning the skills of Dragon Riding."

Thea opened and closed her mouth. Her eyes brightened. I didn't want her to be kicked out—but I didn't want to go either. I couldn't bear the idea of never seeing Kalax again. I stepped forward. "It wasn't her fault, Instructor Mordecai. It was mine. I had this idea about using stars to navigate at night, and we went up to the ridge so I could show her. We weren't…it wasn't…we were talking dragons and flying…and just lost track of time."

Mordecai turned to me, lifting the lantern higher. "So you took it upon yourself to try to teach Cadet Flamma skills you haven't even been taught? Of all the arrogance. I should ask for both of you to be sent home. How do you expect to be Dragon Riders if you cannot manage to follow even the simple rules of the Dragon Academy? What will you do when you have orders to follow and lives depending on you to do what you are asked to do?" He shook his head.

Thea pushed forward, nudging my arm. "It wasn't all Seb's fault. And how can you tell us we should learn everything we can and then yell at us for trying to learn?"

Mordecai's eyes narrowed. He looked from Thea to me and back again. "So you're defending him? You're defending each other?" His mouth curved. "Maybe you will make riders, yet. I admire your loyalty to each other. But this cannot go unpunished. You both will be cleaning out the pony stables for the rest of the month. I want to see you there every morning before breakfast. This is also your second mark against you—one more and both of

169

you will be up before the academy to be sent down." Mordecai stabbed a finger at me. "And since you value night learning so much, you will spend the hours between dinner and bed in the map room studying until I see fit to release you or you graduate. Do you understand?"

Relief washed over me. One more mark was bad, but it wasn't two marks, and us getting thrown out. Still, I wanted to argue with him. Why were we getting a mark against us if we also had to clean out the pony stables and spend hours in the map room— not that I minded that part of it—but I thought it was unfair to have all of that piled on us.

Before I could say anything, Thea put her hand on my arm. "Yes, Instructor. Thank you, Instructor. You've been very just."

I glared at Thea, but she had on her best smile. That seemed to soften Mordecai a little. He gave a nod and stood away from the door. "Off to bed. And if this ever happens again, or your performance is damaged tomorrow by all your late-night antics, remember...you are one mark away from being expelled."

We hurried out of the door. In the main keep, I turned for my room. Thea paused on the steps up to her room and said, her voice quiet, "Seb?"

I glanced at her and nodded. I knew what she was going to say, and it was almost like with Kalax where I knew her thoughts, too, but I only gave a nod and headed for my room. I wasn't willing to face any more duties or punishments added onto my already growing list. One more mark, and both of us were facing the end of our days as cadets—and the loss of ever riding a dragon again.

CHAPTER 18

REVELATIONS

By the time I slipped into my room high in the keep, the matron had already gone to bed. Varla had come back from visiting her folks. She had the lantern burning on the small table between our beds, and she looked up from the book she was reading in bed.

Varla was a curious case at the academy. She was one of the few girls who had ever been chosen by a dragon, but we all knew that her parents didn't want her to fly. They were constantly petitioning the king to free her from duty, and every time she went home she came back looking thin and pale. I could only think her parents were trying to convince her to quit. I'd heard from Ryan that she had performed well at her trials, and she should have graduated into being a fully-fledged Dragon Rider. But then her partner, Ty, broke his leg, and poor Varla was being held in a sort of limbo as the academy and the king's council negotiated with the family over her status. She rarely joined the other cadets in any flying or training, and her dragon—a green— was getting fat from not enough exercise.

Every time I saw her, it struck a shiver of fear into my heart. What would happen if the same thing happened to me? My parents, so far, had supported my becoming a Dragon Rider. But

172

what if something happened to Seb? Would that be excuse enough for others to decide the academy was no place for a girl?

Varla shoved a strand of red hair back. She always had it tied back in a braid. She frowned at me like she wasn't sure she liked me any more than I liked her. I nodded, shouldering off the cloak and skirt and blouse I'd borrowed. I could feel Varla's eyes on me, but she never asked where I'd been. Her eyes looked rimmed by red, and her freckles stood out on her pale skin. I wondered if her parents had been after her to leave the academy again.

I also wondered if I was now on Instructor Mordecai's personal hit-list. Maybe I'd end up like Varla, a permanent cadet.

Putting down her book, Varla gestured to the skirt I'd left on the floor. "What's up with that? Doesn't your family give you nice things to wear?"

I sat down on my bed and stared at her. It seemed to be a night to tear down walls, first with Seb and now with Varla. I'd taken Seb's side against an instructor—and Mordecai had approved of that. Maybe it was time for me to stop trying to be the best and start trying to be one with my fellow cadets.

Besides, what could it hurt?

I told her about how I'd gone to hear the gypsy stories, how I feared there was something terribly wrong, that a danger might be approaching and I had gone to find answers but had only managed to get into trouble for it. At the end of it all, I admitted, "I'm afraid I'll never become a Dragon Rider if Instructor Mordecai has his way."

Varla sniffed and rubbed her nose. "Sounds like maybe you shouldn't be so hard on your partner. He sounds like one of the good ones to me." Her shoulders slumped and her eyes—they were green I noticed—took on a haunted look. I suddenly wondered if maybe her dragon had dumped Ty for a reason— maybe he wasn't one of the good partners.

"What do you mean?" I asked.

She shook her head. "Sounds like Seb puts you ahead of the rules. Not many will do that. Maybe it's because he's your navigator—he's trying to help you find your way, even on the ground, isn't he?"

I winced. A stab of guilt churned in my stomach. It had been my idea to go out of the academy. Tonight was my fault. But Seb had been trying to find a path for both of us. "Uh, yeah," I said.

"Well, then, maybe you should think about that. Maybe he's just really trying to help you." Varla put her book on the table, turned over and said, "Turn off the light when you're ready."

I did. But I lay there, staring at the darkness, thinking about how I had acted toward both Varla and Seb. I'd wanted them to be what I wanted—what I needed. I'd wanted them to stay out of my way. I hadn't thought about how I could be helping them. That left me with a lot to think about. And for some reason the darkness tonight seemed to press down on me with extra fears.

*   *   *

The next day I dragged myself to meet Seb in the stables so we could muck out the stalls of the mountain ponies. Seb, however, was already up, and whistling cheerfully as he moved from stall to stall, tossing out wet straw and picking through the clean bits.

"You have a way with animals," I told him, yawning and grabbing a pitchfork to use on the straw. I didn't mind the smell. Dragons smelled like fire—like some kind of incense you might burn. Or at least Kalax did. The ponies had an earthy smell, and I liked how they nosed my pockets for treats. But they loved Seb— they nudged him with their heads, and stood next to him, like he was their best friend ever.

Seb stopped and looked at me. "I never thought about it that way. I thought that maybe it was just that I got along with Kalax."

I could see why Sebastian had been born a navigator. I watched him as he worked and saw that he had a way of talking to the ponies that made them feel at ease. It was the same kind of thing he had with Kalax, something that he had taught me to sense, but I knew I would never be able to replicate it in full. It was a strange gift, and something I told myself to think about, because the other navigators didn't seem to be on such easy and intimate terms with their mounts. I also kept thinking about the gypsy's stories.

Once I'd fallen asleep, I'd had bad dreams of a darkness that smothered me, sucking the warmth and light from inside me, leaving nothing behind—not even a memory of who I'd been. The dreams had left me tired, and by the time we'd finished the stalls, I was almost wishing I could go back to bed.

But training today was a synchronized flying mission where we had to fly with the other cadets and find specific locations that had been flagged. I found that things went better than I expected.

For once, I didn't feel the gut-crunching panic I usually did in the air. Seb was almost anticipating every turn I asked for. I used the telescope to spot directions and gave instructions, but Seb was already ready before I'd asked. It was like the little time we'd had last night in the woods had bonded us. Or maybe it was just sharing a punishment. But Kalax too, seemed to fly much more smoothly for us both. If we did as well as Jensen and Wil, we'd be in the top of the class along with those two.

We finished the training and turned back for home. As we came in to land on our platform, my good mood plummeted. Instructor Mordecai stood on the nearest tower, unmistakably staring and scowling at us. I knew then that it might not matter how good we did if Mordecai was determined to see us fail. I sighed heavily as I helped Seb dismount and started to unhook our harnesses.

"Hey, now," Beris called out, stepping up to our platform with a big grin. "Don't go trading roles with your navigator, Thea." He waved at the links and straps of Kalax's harness.

My face heated. It was usually the navigator's job to clean the gear, but there was no reason a protector couldn't help.

Beris' grin widened. "Who knows what might happen next— you might start forgetting to wash your hair." Beris nudged Syl, who started to grin, too. I shouldered my way past Beris, carrying the harness while Seb carried the saddle. I kept wishing Beris and Syl would go away.

"Look, I'm helping my navigator," I said, tired and irritable. Beris was my friend, but the way that he constantly went after Seb was starting to annoy me. "Maybe you should help your navigator too, so maybe Syl won't have your dragon flying like a drunk hedgehog all the time!" I snapped. Syl, Will and Jensen, who all stood nearby now, laughed.

Beris just flushed a deep shade of crimson.

Moving up next to me, Seb said, his voice soft, "Thanks." I glanced at him, annoyed with him, too, and feeling a little awkward for taking his side. "It's not about you, it's just about flying. We've got to be able to fly well." I gave him a firm nod.

"Yeah." Seb's smile faded as we put away the dragon saddle

and harnesses. He looked up at me and said, "If things ever get bad, I mean like in the stories we heard the other night," he waved a hand, "I'll look after you, Thea."

I shook my head and started out of the saddle room. "Dummy, I'm the protector. It'll be me looking after you." I headed out into the sunshine. I didn't want to think about dark things or trouble brewing, or anything but trying to keep my focus on graduating. But warmth spread through me when I thought of Seb's words, and a chill when I thought of those stories about the Darkening.

CHAPTER 19

OF MAPS AND MINES

Thea stood up for me against Beris and Syl and Shakasta. I kept thinking about that as I crossed the chilly training area to the observation tower door and started up the stairs.

I almost didn't mind that I had to spend the hours after dinner up in the map room at the top of observatory tower. I guess that I was still riding high on the events of the day.

Did Thea taking my side mean something? Was she starting to believe in me? Did she have some trust in me? My steps slowed as I climbed the stairs, one after the other after the endless other. Everything in me was exhausted, from my toes to the ends of my hair. I thought back to the way Thea had so fearlessly crossed the ridge with me, the warmth of Arkady and Sansha's fire, and how she had stood with me. But I wasn't sure this change was going to last.

Reaching the top, I stepped inside to see Merik, collecting scrolls and maps and sorting them out. Like always, the room smelled like paper and dust. I was surprised to see Merik here this late, but I didn't usually see him down in the training area either. He glanced up, adjusted his optics and asked, "Hey, Seb, what brings you up here so late?"

"Work duty from Mordecai." I groaned and flopped into a chair. The wood groaned under my weight.

Merik laughed. "Ah, well, best of luck to you. He's a stickler for his work duties." Merik went back to his work, humming a cheery tune.

Getting up, I went to help him and asked how he was doing with training. He shrugged. "Actually, Commander Hegarty said my progress was looking good. But…well, Hegarty is nice most of the time. I'm still hoping that maybe a dragon will choose me again. Hegarty said they won't give me my place—not protector or navigator—until I have a dragon pick me again."

"What about your eyesight?" I asked.

Merik reached out and tapped one of the telescopes that was only as large as a handheld dagger. "I've got an idea to alter a pair of these into the goggles. Then I just need to find a fellow rider, one who doesn't have a navigator—and a dragon who will take me."

"I thought a dragon will only choose once?"

Merik shook his head. "It's not common, but, well, Hegarty told me about a dragon he knew who dumped its riders—both of them. The dragon decided he didn't like its riders, and wouldn't stay in the enclosure to breed either, but went out and chose new riders. Two of them. The academy had to take them on—the dragon wouldn't let them not do so—and they became two of the best. You've heard of Hollis and Hollis—brothers, the dragon chose that second time. So…I've got hope. Now can you go get me that map over there?"

Merik started up a ladder to put away some scrolls. I headed over to the table and saw that Merik had spread out a map of the mountains to the north. I glanced at him. "Is there a reason you have this out?"

Merik came down the ladder. "No reason…just…" He put a finger to push his optics back in place. "Well, the mountains have never been mapped completely accurately because there are so many passes and trails, and…well, it's just I've started to hear stories."

My skin chilled. "Of trouble?"

He glanced at me and nodded. "You too? They sound like just stories, but I thought it wouldn't hurt to take a look at what's out there, and since I can't fly…"

"You can see what we know from maps." I nodded. Spreading out the map, I could see my friend was right—a lot of the mountain areas in both elevation maps and action maps were little more than white blobs with dotted lines of trails. I was willing to bet the storms kept most Dragon Riders from being able to get a good look at those northern mountain.

I glanced at the maps again. "I'm not seeing any villages. I thought folks lived in the north."

Merik nodded. "Of course they do."

"So why don't we have maps of those places?" I stared at one map after the next, none of them had any villages marked.

"Yes, there's got to be one here," Merik said, pulling out another map.

But there was nothing. No great passes marked. No settlements. No major towns or villages. I stared at the empty maps and I wondered why anyone would even want to attack this area—there was nothing here of worth.

"Wait a minute..." Merik leaned over the map he'd pulled out. "You see that?" He pointed to a different colour marked onto the map of the mountains.

"Yeah? What is it?"

"That's the mark for a mine. Look, they're scattered over these mountains."

"And where you have mines...there should be people to work them. And villages." I stared at the map. "It's like the Dragon Riders who mapped this area couldn't see them." My voice dropped low. "Or couldn't recall what they'd seen. But what's so special about rock and ore? Why would anyone want these mines?" I glanced at Merik, eyebrows lifted high.

"Gold and silver? Copper? Riches?" Merik asked. He shook his head. "But I've seen one of the old scrolls that said there weren't any precious metals up in the north mountains. Just tin."

"Merik, have you ever heard of magic stones?"

He grinned. "You mean the Dragon Egg Stone stories? Sure, everyone knows those."

I shook my head. "No, I mean have you heard they're real— that the Dragon Riders ever used magic?"

He shook his head. "Just in the old legends I've heard. I don't think—well, my old gran used to say magic has a cost, and for every bit of good it can do, it can do bad as well. But Dragon Rider history—at least the written history—doesn't have any mention of magic. It's all just text books about dragons and training. No one seemed to have thought to write anything down about the other riders, or even the history of our academy. We just have the stories and songs of past feats of bravery."

"And that's enough to make sure no one would go to war with the Dragon Riders of Torvald, especially over something as worthless as tin, but if there really were magic stones…?" I let the words trail off. If there were such stones, why didn't the Dragon Riders still have them? Why didn't anyone know of them? I shook my head and put a hand on the maps. I might not be able to find the answers, but I knew where to start. "We should find out where the most northern village or town is located. There's got to be a record of it." I scanned the maps, but Merik headed over to one of the shelves and pulled out a heavy book.

He put the book on the table with a thud. "King's Village." He turned to a page that listed villages and nearby mineral deposits, written out by some long-dead scholar of Torvald.

I leaned over the book and read from the page. "It says here the township known as King's Village was actually a little bit bigger than a village. It was one of the first villages the monarchy of Torvald set up outside the mountain citadel. It was to the north, but only two days by horse and five by foot. The village mined raw ore, but mostly tin." I glanced at Merik. "Have you ever heard of King's Village?"

Merik shook his head. "No. But then…I don't know much about the north. It's always just called that—the north. Do you think all of this has something to do with the mines there?"

I shook my head. I could sense something wasn't right, but I couldn't quite see what. There still had to be a piece missing. "We need to tell Thea. She should tell the prince about this." I waved at the maps.

"Tell the prince what?" said a voice from the doorway. Both Merik and I spun. Commander Hegarty stood in the doorway, filling the space and frowning as he smoothed his moustache. He could move very quietly when he wanted to because I certainly hadn't heard him coming.

I was struck dumb suddenly, my mouth dried and my breathing hitched. Who was I to presume that I had found out some important secret or threat? I pulled in a breath. "The maps—they…they're not showing any villages." I winced. That sounded a lame reason to speak to the prince even to me.

The commander put his stare on me, his eyes stern. "I heard from Instructor Mordecai that you had been causing some problems, Sebastian. I wanted to come up here and talk to you, and I fear he may have been right after all. Are you here looking to make trouble?"

"No, sir," I stiffened. "It was just, ah, you see…we're worried about rumors of villages in the mountains…" I let the words trail. I sounded an idiot, babbling and making up ridiculous stories. A child chasing after legends, not a cadet out to become a Dragon Rider.

The commander's eyebrows lifted high. He shook his head. "I see how it must be a big change, coming up from Monger's Lane to the academy." He put a hand on my shoulder. "Your excitement is admirable, cadet, and I understand wanting to make a name for yourself. But perhaps you need to concentrate on your studies a bit more and focus on just learning how to be a cadet. Learn how to fly first, and then you may think up plans to save the realm."

"Yes, sir." I blushed hot and stared down at the toes of my

boot.

He put a hand on my shoulder. I looked up and saw a smile ease his face. "Although, that does not mean all legends are false, nor that all passions are stupid. What are we doing here, if not trying to live a fantasy of riding dragons? Best sometimes to let trouble find you instead of you looking for it," Hegarty said, giving me an odd look.

Is he trying to tell me I might be right about my worries? I thought maybe the commander couldn't say that he believed in rumors of trouble. He was Commander of the Dragon Academy. He had a responsibility to see to it the academy ran smoothly. And I was just a lowly cadet. He might even be sworn to secrecy about certain matters.

"But there is also good news, for Merik, at least." Hegarty turned to Merik. "It has been decided to see if Ferdinania will accept you as a rider."

"Ferdinania!" Merik said. He blinked. "But isn't she…isn't she Ty's dragon? And Varla's?"

Hegarty huffed out a breath. "Ty will not be returning to the academy. It was discovered he was not treating his dragon well. That was why Ferdinania put him on the ground. But we do not know if Ferdinania will accept you, and if she does, well…we will see about what comes next then."

"Varla," I said, repeating the name. That was the girl who roomed with Thea. I remembered Thea saying Varla was a navigator—so was Merik. How could a dragon go out with two navigators and no protector?

The commander slapped Merik's shoulder. "Congratulations. Report tomorrow to the platforms and we'll see if Ferdinania will have you and Varla or not."

He turned, but before he left, the commander put a hard stare on me. "Cadet, I'm hoping you will prove to everyone how good a Dragon Rider you will be. But I caution you, have a care with your rides. You'll soon be able to take longer flights, and perhaps you'll be able to help Merik get used to the skies." He gave a nod and left.

I wondered if he had been telling me in his own way—and without coming out and saying it outright—that I should go ahead and continue looking into the rumors of troubles in the north.

CHAPTER 20

LEGEND OF THE EGGS

I heard from Seb about how Ty would not return to the academy, and that Ferdinania might pick Merik as rider. Seb seemed excited for Merik, but I couldn't help but think about poor Ty. I hadn't known him well, but it had to be hard for any cadet to have to quit—to have to live without ever flying again. I shivered at the idea. That would be more than awful, it would be like having to live without an arm or a leg.

We all headed to the platforms to watch Ferdinania land—to see if she would take Merik or not. He seemed nervous, shifting from foot to foot, and even Varla looked paler than ever, her freckles standing out on her cheeks like dots. But it turned out to not be that big a deal. Ferdinania landed—she had to be the biggest blue I'd ever seen and her platform creaked under her weight. She stretched her nose out, snuffled Varla, tipped her head to one side, and stared at Merik with gold-green eyes. The moment seemed to go on forever, and then she blew a puff of smoke at Merik through her nose. He coughed, and in the next moment Ferdinania nudged him with her nose, too. And that was that.

I had thought a dragon choosing a rider would take more time—or that there would be a ceremony or something. But it was just done and Ferdinania settled on her platform, wrapping her tail around her as if she was happy. Seb nudged me and leaned close as Merik and Varla stood with Ferdinania. "She likes him."

I glanced at Seb. "How do you know? Are you sure you're not just saying that because you like Merik?" Seb grinned. When I looked back at Merik, I could see he was scratching Ferdinania in just the same spot Seb scratched Kalax. I narrowed my eyes at Seb. "You told him about that spot—that's Kalax's favorite."

Seb shrugged, like it was no big deal. But I wondered if Seb had given Merik just a small edge to help him win over Ferdinania.

The next week passed with more and more flight training. Varla and Merik were going to have to go through the trials again to sort out their positions, but until then they were swapping spots as navigator and protector. It was weird to see them do that, but it seemed to be working for Ferdinania. The only chance I had to talk to Seb was in the mornings when we had to sweep out the stables.

Seb told me about the mines on the maps, and how the maps hadn't shown any villages in the mountains to the north. I didn't think it was that weird, but maybe there was something to the idea that someone wanted those mines in the north for something. Seb wanted me to talk to the prince again, but Justin was off on a patrol of the western shores with his squadron. I didn't know when he would get back and I was starting to think the only way we'd find out what was going on in the north was by flying there.

When I told Seb that on our last morning of cleaning stables, he just stared at me. I stopped cleaning a stall and leaned against one of the ponies, fuzzy now loosing its winter coat. "What?" I asked, staring at Seb. "You were the one who snuck out of the academy that first night as if it was nothing. Now you think a flight is a bad thing? Don't you want to try and defend the people of Torvald?"

Seb frowned. "Of course I do—but one more mark against us and we're both out."

I shook my head. "I know that, but I'm talking about a cleared, extended flight. That's all. We're going to be in the advanced trials soon, and we could ask the commander's permission to get in extra flying practice. And if we don't look into this, who will?"

Seb's mouth pulled even lower. "If we get expelled, your life will be ruined. I don't want to be to blame for that."

I rolled my eyes. The pony I was leaning on shifted, I patted him, sneezed at the dust off his coat and straightened. "Oh, and your life wouldn't be ruined if we were sent down?"

Turning back to the stall he was working on, Seb hunched a shoulder. "I'd just go back to the smithy. I never thought I'd be a

Dragon Rider anyway."

I huffed out a breath. "So you wouldn't miss Kalax, would you?" Or me, I thought. "Well, go ahead and stay here and clean stalls if that's all you want to do!" Slamming out of the stables, I threw down my rake. I was starting to feel trapped. There was nothing I could do to convince Prince Justin of the trouble that might be coming right now, and I was getting tired of always being on my best behavior since I never knew when Instructor Mordecai might be watching. Now even Seb was getting all stuffy. He'd picked a fine time to start being the perfect cadet.

If there was any consolation, the advanced trials were about to start. That would mean actual combat on dragons. Riders would be pitched against each other, using padded arrows to simulate combat. I knew that I was one of the better archers and Seb was one of the better navigators, so we should be able to win some favor with the sour Mordecai by performing well.

I knew I shouldn't leave the rest of the stables to Seb, but I just couldn't go back in there when I was still mad at him. I headed up the top of the stone walls. Varla and Merik were out on Ferdinania, trying to get extra practice in.

Varla was starting to ride more often as the protector, but I could see by the way she sat that she wasn't really comfortable in the role. I watched Ferdinania dive and turn. I heard Varla give a yell, and Merik a laugh. They were both so eager to learn and were training so hard, but Merik's skills in the air were terrible and while Varla knew all the technical points about flying, she didn't look like she really trusted her dragon or her partner.

I cringed when I saw them flopping through another turn. I also thought about my own lack of trust in Seb. But, honestly, how could I trust him when he kept changing on me?

Ferdinania came in for a landing on her platform, graceful even though she was huge. She let out a small puff of smoke— she seemed to like doing that. Varla dismounted, and Merik waved at her, telling her to go on to breakfast and that he would handle unsaddling Ferdinania.

"Hey, Varla!" I said, waving at her as she started for the stairs. "I was just headed to the kitchens to grab something. Nice flying."

She fell into step with me, rubbing her shoulder with one hand. "By heavens, I don't think I am ever going to get the hang of these new saddles."

"New? You haven't been here that long."

She flipped her red braid back over her shoulder. "Well, the saddles on the barrels are a lot easier than the ones on a living, breathing dragon."

I had to smile at that. Varla probably had spent more time riding the fake dragons than anyone. I punched her shoulder.

"Hey, you had extra time to learn strategies most of us haven't tried yet. You'll do great at the trials."

She wrinkled her nose. "Merik and I have to do trials—and then advanced trials right after that. The instructors still don't know how we'll fit best on Ferdinania. At least she doesn't mind us swapping spots." She let out a sigh. "But sometimes, I almost wish I could go back to hiding in my books and just reading my way through the library."

Reading...reading her way through the library. I thought about that and an idea lodged in my brain. Varla probably knew more history than anyone, even Merik.

Walking across the training area, I asked, "Say, Varla, in all of your years of reading, did you ever come across anything about tin mines being...oh, I don't know, special somehow?"

"Mines? Tin mines?" Varla stopped looked at me. "Like under-the-ground mines? You do realize we are at a flying school, right?"

I tugged on her sleeve and we headed into the kitchens. It was late for breakfast. The great hall would be empty. But I snagged two rolls for us, and Varla grabbed apples. We found a quiet corner past where the staff were cleaning dishes and drying mugs. Giving one roll to Varla, I told her, "It's just that, well, Seb found something odd on the maps, the ones of the northern mountains."

"Odd? What kind of odd?"

Between bites of roll, I told her about the stories of villages disappearing, and how the maps didn't show any villages near the northern mines. "Seb thinks there's something odd about the mines—they're all tin mines, he said."

Varla bit into an apple. When she finished chewing, she shrugged. "Well, I've read everything there is about dragon riding, flying and the history of the academy, as well as most of the myths. But I don't remember reading anything about rocks and tunnels." She wrinkled her nose. "There was one old book, all about how to find the alloy for Dragon Rider's armor, and it had the Legend of the Eggs."

I knew the legend she spoke of. Every child learned it, and I thought even Seb must know it.

Hundreds of years ago, in the early days of the dragons and the humans becoming friends, one wizard found magical stones shaped like dragon eggs that had been buried deep in natural caverns.

"Mines," I said, thinking of the old stories that I had not heard in years. The Legend of the Eggs was one story my mother hadn't minded me hearing—it had never given me bad dreams.

Varla reached for another apple. "You going to eat this?" I shook my head. She nodded, bit in, and said around a mouthful,

"Although—that's not where you get real dragon eggs. Dragons lay only one egg at a time and they prefer soft nests—they like deer-hide lining or sheepskin, and they prefer to build the nest in a high spot, far above the ground. I read that in another book, The Complete Care of Dragons by A. E. Tivlet." She smiled and bit into her apple again.

"If I remember the old stories, these dragon stones, the ones that seemed like eggs, were each of a different colour, and each one had a different power."

Varla nodded. "The light green one could control the mind, a black could make a person have skin thick as a dragon's scale. The white one...I can't remember what it could do."

"Wasn't it healing?" I said.

"I think that's right. Then there was a stone the colour of the deepest moss—that was named the Dragon Stone, and it had the powers to bind all the other stones so that one person could use them all—I think it also gave immortality, invincibility, and it was a stone that could kill." Varla finished her apple. "I never could see why you need all the other stones, if one had the powers of them all, but it's typical of myths. Stories get woven together with just a little fact. After all, a stone only kills if you hit someone with it."

I let out a breath. "How can you get Dragon Rider armor from a tin mines?"

Varla shrugged. "The book didn't go into that, but I don't think you can. It was implied that Dragon Rider armor is made of several metals—the writer didn't give any kind of recipes—so I think maybe you have to have special ore, and it's found in the same places you'll find tin."

I wondered if Seb knew how to make Dragon Rider armor. His father was a smithy, but then not all smiths worked armor. Some, I knew, only worked in iron, and some only in the hardened steel for weapons. I also remembered back to the stories that Arkady had told us—how the Dragon Riders had defeated the Darkening with magic stones.

Varla rose and I did as well, and before she could leave I asked her, "This book—did it say anything about the Dragon Riders using magic stones?"

"For what? As weapons?" she shook her head. "I've never seen anything about Dragon Riders using magic stones—just the Legends of the Eggs. Frankly, it seemed like a child's tale to me. But then, it was really hard to read because it was written down a long, long time ago."

The Dragon Horn sounded to call us to training. Varla gave me a nod and hurried out. I followed more slowly. Were these stories connected—and were they true? I thought about the villages that were not on the maps the way they should be. Did someone want those mines—those places—left forgotten for a reason? I knew I had to find Seb—not just for training, but to tell him what I'd learned from Varla. He'd have to see that now we had to fly north. We'd find out what was really going on, find some evidence we could show to others and then we could come back and make sure something was done about it.

CHAPTER 21

ADVANCED TRIALS

Thea pounced on me to tell me of a conversation she'd had with Varla. Unfortunately, she wanted to talk while we were flying Kalax. With Thea yelling at me, I kept getting confused about what to do and we almost ran into Jenson and Wil's big green dragon. A fast move from Kalax saved us, but nearly threw us from the saddles. When training was over, Instructor Mordecai stomped over and gave us two extra hours back on riding the fake-dragon barrels. I gave a groan, bit off a complaint and said, "Yes, sir." I had learned from Thea that it was always better to swallow your words.

The extra training meant neither Thea nor I had time to do anything. Every time we tried to see Commander Hegarty to get him to clear a long flight north for us, Instructor Mordecai seemed to pop up with something more for us to learn. If it wasn't more map reading, it was flag reading, or it was archery down in the training area, or it was sparring, or it was scrubbing out the main hall. Every night I fell into bed, aching and exhausted.

The day of the advanced trials found me nervous, mulling over more than just the test ahead of us. I was thinking about what Thea had told me about the legend of the magical stones. I'd never heard those stories before—Thea couldn't believe I hadn't. But I told her how my da hated any kind of stories.

She'd stared at me, then said, her voice small and soft, "Mother hated me hearing the stories of the Darkening. They gave me nightmares. They still do."

I nodded. I was having bad dreams too, about Monger's Lane vanishing, and I'd go there, calling out for my da, but no one would answer.

The feeling was growing in me that something was very wrong. All the stories kept mixing in my mind into a terrible picture—what if the mines of the north were where these stones of power were buried? Or what if the ore in these mines let you make more than Dragon Armor—what if it could be used to make weapons?

I shook my head over the ideas, sure they must be just tied to my bad dreams. Even if something was wrong up north, it was up to the prince and his Dragon Riders—not a cadet—to sort it out.

Besides, I needed to focus on the advance trials.

Instructor Mordecai was looking for any reason to boot me—and Thea—out, and I wasn't going to disappoint Commander Hegarty again. I'd vowed not to be the reason for Thea getting expelled from the academy, and that meant I needed to stay away from harebrained, silly ideas like stealing a horse and riding off to the mountains in search of mythical, magical eggs. I needed to keep Thea from that, too. The fear that she might just go off on her own haunted me. I had to keep an eye on her—she was my partner and I had to try to protect her as much as I could. We are a team.

I heard an annoyed grumble rattle underneath me from Kalax. She could sense how I was distressed. I sent calming thoughts down and into her, reassuring her that everything would be well.

It won't be if you think in two places at once.

Her reply came back clear and sharp, and I was surprised. It wasn't often that a dragon managed to concentrate enough to use our language. But Kalax was special like that I knew, and she was getting better at reading me. She learned fast.

You are right, I thought at the dragon. Head in the game. Head in the game!

We were perched on the edge of our wooden platforms, waiting to begin our advanced trial. This would be an actual combat trial, one of the tests where we would take to the skies to attack and defend in a controlled battle. Thea's arrows were tipped with bulbous wads of leather and canvas, all held in a quiver that had ink at the bottom. Our colour was red, to match Kalax, just as Merik and Varla's ink would be a dark blue to match Ferdinania, and Jensen and Wil's would be green to match their dragon, and so on. At the end of the day, when we were recalled to the academy, they would count which dragon had received the most hits, where they were and the instructors would review the battle, our successes and our failures.

My harness held me snug to Kalax's back. I had on a leather helmet, goggles and a thicker leather jerkin that acted almost like armor. I had my hands on the pulleys and handles that would help guide Kalax's wings. Thea, behind me, had a much harder task of using the rope link as well as her seat harness so she could stand up, reach over and defend more of Kalax and myself should she need to.

I breathed, closing my eyes to the beating of Kalax's large heart.

The Dragon Horn blew and the dragons leaped from their platforms, peeling off in different direction across the sky. The rules of the advanced trials were simple: the goal of each of two teams was to capture the other team's flag while defending their own flag. Thea and I had Varla and Merik on our team—Varla and Merik had finished their trials, and Varla had been assigned as a protector and Merik as navigator. Merik had told me Varla had immediately stepped away from the instructors and had thrown up. I was just hoping they'd be okay in the advanced trials.

Each team had a short amount of time to fly away from each other, safe from attack. When the second horn sounded, the trials proper would begin.

Kalax seemed to know what was happening. I nudged her in the direction of the mountain top to defend our target. She had rarely been in the air with this many other dragons, and I could tell that she was excited and worried at the same time. Her tendency was to beat her powerful leathery wings to gain as much height as possible over the others to be able to hold a position of superiority, looking down on the pack since she was younger, still growing and right now smaller. I encouraged her in those instincts.

I turned to cast a quick look back to Thea. She had one hand on the handle of her harness and held her bow in the other. She was scanning the horizon for the nearest dragons, ready to notch one of our red-tinted arrows at short notice. She looked determined, calm even…and serious.

Remind me never to get on the wrong side of her. But that was exactly what I was about to do if she kept insisting we had to fly north to investigate those mines.

The second Dragon Horn sounded. The trials had begun.

*   *   *

Kalax roared as another arrow swept past her left shoulder, shot by Tenzer on his small, yellow dragon. I could feel Kalax's heartbeat thrumming fast and hard. She felt like she was on the edge of spitting fire. I put a hand on her neck to calm her. Fire wasn't supposed to be part of the advanced trials. Besides, Tenzer had missed. But that didn't mean that he wasn't going to try again.

"Right," Thea shouted. I turned to see the blue body of Beris' dragon soar up vertically past me. He was a stouter dragon then Kalax, and his powerful wings buffeted the side of our red, rocking her in the sky.

Taking advantage of our floundering, Beris shot an arrow down at us. I couldn't turn Kalax in time. It was going to hit us dead center!

I sensed rather than saw Thea throw herself out of her saddle, a shield strapped to her arm extended. The arrow clanged into her shield and fell away. Thea was still attached to her harness by a line of rope, but she looked pale.

Kalax regained her balance. I turned her, giving Thea a shot at the bigger blue. A red arrow arced through the air, but in the rush of wings I couldn't see if it hit or not.

"Below," Thea shouted. I could hear from her voice that she was both terrified and elated by the action. I swung around see that Tenzer's yellow was climbing up and almost directly below us. Under his helmet I could see a savage look of glee on his face.

"Hold on!" I sent a command to Kalax to dive as if she was

fishing the lake for food. She half-somersaulted in mid-air, tucking her wings in close to her body and fell like a shooting star.

I heard a yell behind me and turned to see Thea hanging on to her harness, her legs tumbling in the air behind her. Kalax purred with savage satisfaction and kept dropping. Wind tore at my face and goggles, pushing me into my saddle.

Wait for it…wait for it, I thought to Kalax. I knew she trusted me completely. The ground rose to meet us. We flashed past Tenzer's dragon and Beris, heading in a seeming death dive toward the fields and woodland below.

"Now," I shouted and thought at the same time, and felt the incredible resistance as Kalax pushed out her wings, using the sudden lift to soar forward like a speeding hawk on the wind. It was a classic escape or attack move, but one that was dangerous to pull off because it relied on the navigator and dragon holding their nerve for the maximum amount of time to ensure the most momentum when they finally caught the air current.

Trees and hills zipped past us. Sheep and horses fled from our approach. Kalax's shadow flashed across the river and rocks below.

"There—northwest," Thea yelled, pointing to where two dragons were curling and coiling across the sky. It looked like Jensen and Merik were each in a race to get to the mountain top and the flag, seemingly not firing in an attempt to outpace each other.

One of the blues—the smaller, more sinuous one—broke ahead of the larger red. That was Jensen's dragon gaining the lead. I didn't want anyone to win apart from us, but I still mentally wished Merik and Varla good luck as we soared upward. And then I saw Ferdinania turn and snap at her harness—her flight suddenly veered into erratic circles.

Something was wrong.

Ferdinania started to lose altitude, falling downward in a spiral with stops and starts that had to be jarring Merik and Varla. The blue dove toward the deeply wooded ravines below our target mountain.

"What's wrong?" Thea called out.

I shook my head. I didn't know. But maybe I could find out. I told Kalax to follow as close as she dared. I closed my eyes, concentrating on the wind, the feel of the dragon beneath me…and then reaching out to the dragons nearby.

I opened my eyes and stretched a hand toward Ferdinania. It was a natural instinct. I had never seen another navigator do this, but somehow I could feel Ferdinania in the same way that I could feel Kalax's. But Ferdinania's mind seemed much less distinct. If Kalax was like a burning bonfire right beneath me, Ferdinania would be a bright candle in the room next door. But feelings stirred within me.

Pain. Fear. Distrust.

I could sense Ferdinania was not thinking and acting like a trained dragon, but more like a wild dragon. She was distrustful of the humans around her and uncomfortable in her harness.

Dragon sickness, Kalax's voice whispered in my mind. Harder to remember what humans want us to be.

I'd heard about Dragon Sickness. It was the main reason why the academy kept the dragons in the enclosure rather than building stables for them at the academy. Older dragons could come down with a sickness, like swamp fever, that affected their minds. Younger dragons could get it, too, and I wondered if Ferdinania had caught it from being on her own for so long, without any riders who could look after her. I'd heard this wild spirit could be passed on to young dragons.

"She's sick!" I shouted at Thea. "We have to help!"

Before I could say more, Ferdinania roared and plummeted out of the sky in a wild roll. I knew she was seeking to dislodge her riders—like a wild dragon. That meant she hadn't really bonded with them.

This was bad news. She could easily kill Varla and Merik by bucking them out of their saddles. If they somehow survived to the ground, she might view them as prey.

The warming presence of Kalax's mind against my own stirred. Ferdinania brood-friend, she thought, and I agreed. We swooped down after them.

The hole in the forest canopy looked ugly to me, all broken branches and crushed twigs. A path of destruction from Ferdinania tearing through the forest. There was no sign of the dragon or her riders.

"There!" Thea pointed. I turned and saw a harness and saddle hanging entangled in the trees. It looked like they'd been brushed into the branches—but where were the riders?

"Oh no." We swooped lower, and faint voices rose up from the ground. I looked down and saw a flash of white from between the trees. A river snaked through the bottom of a ravine. Next to it, on the rocky shore, Varla and Merik jumped up and down, Varla waving a white scarf to attract our attention.

"Thank heavens they're alive," Thea said. With a nod, I asked Kalax to swoop down and land. She did so, stretching out her wings and legs like a swan and landing on the waters of the mountain river. She sent up a huge wave before her.

Kalax paddled to the shore. I unclipped my harness and jumped down. Merik headed over to his, his goggles pushed up. He looked tired. His leather jerkin was torn, and his breeches stained with green, but otherwise he seemed okay. "I thought that we were gonna die for sure."

"She went mad. Dragon Sickness!" Varla kicked at the sand, frowning and unhappy. She clutched her arms to her sides and I figured she was going to be more than bruised by that landing.

"I know," I said. The sand and rocks of the mountain river crunched against my boots. I hugged first Merik, then Varla. "You're a new partnership, she must be stressed—she didn't fully bond with you. Maybe this is why they hate for dragons to try and choose a second time." I was as worried for the dragon as much as I was for our friends.

"Well, thank goodness you're alive," Thea said. She'd unfastened her harness and had climbed down from her saddle. "We can get you on our dragon and take you back to the academy."

"What about the trial? The mountain?" Merik shook his head. "We'll be disqualified for sure. And…and I don't want to go back without Ferdinania."

I glanced from him to Varla and let out a breath. I hoped they would trust me. "There might be another way."

Varla and Merik swapped a look—they were getting to be better partners than Thea and me, and then Varla asked, "What? We'll try anything."

I wet my lips. "I...I can sense the thoughts of dragons—their feelings. I think that I can use that to help Ferdinania..."

Merik started to shake his head. With his eyes narrowed, he looked like he didn't believe me. Varla looked from me to Thea. "Can he really do that?" she asked.

Thea shrugged. "He has got a way with animals."

Animals? No! Dragons! Kalax's voice appeared in my mind.

I glanced at Kalax, who was searching the sky now, snuffling softly. That gave me an idea. I held out a hand. "Give me a piece of your clothes, each of you...something I can use to remind Ferdinania that she really did choose you. "Thea, can you help them get their saddles and harnesses down from the trees, ready for when we come back."

Reluctantly, Merik pulled off his jerkin then shrugged off his tunic. He put his torn jerkin back on. Varla gave me the scarf she had been waving. I tied each garment to my belt with a leather thong. Kalax, I knew, could find Ferdinania's scent—dragons often used scent to hunt. Once we found her, both Kalax and I could reach out to her with calming and reassuring thoughts, and we'd use the clothing to remind her how she had chosen her riders by their scent.

Or she might just try to rip my head off.

Kalax huffed a breath at that thought. I will not allow.

I smiled and turned to Thea. "If I'm not back by evening, make camp here and try to get back to the academy in the morning when the light is good." Thea put a hand on my arm. "Seb, we could fly back to the academy for help—right now." I shook my head. "The longer Ferdinania stays on her own, the harder it's going to be to get her to shake the sickness. She needs our help, or Varla and Merik might lose her forever. I've got to go after her."

Kalax chirruped her agreement. I gave Thea a nod and a smile. She stepped back. "I just hope you're doing the right thing."

I climbed up into my saddle. "I do, too."

CHAPTER 22

WHAT ARE HEROES MADE OF?

I watched Seb and Kalax rise up into the sky. I didn't know if I would ever do this—ride off after a dragon with the sickness like that. His bravery shocked me, and left me feeling embarrassed for the way I had once treated him, as if he was weak. He clearly wasn't. Turning away from where he and Kalax had been in the river, I headed back to Varla and Merik.

With her face pale and her freckles standing out, and her mouth pressed into a flat line, Varla looked upset. She seemed to be trying to hide it. Merik was limping a little and watching the sky, his eyes dark and worried behind his huge, odd goggles. I felt for both of them. If Ferdinania rejected them as her riders, they wouldn't get another chance.

My throat tightened and my stomach knotted. If I'd been here, brushed off by my dragon, I didn't think I'd be as calm as either of these two. It was important to do something with my life, to show my father and everyone else that I was born to be a Dragon Rider.

"Can he really do it?" Varla said, picking up a stone to skip across the surface of the river.

"You haven't seen him with Kalax. He's got a gift that I don't understand." I nudged her arm. "Come on, let's go get your saddles and harness."

I started for the trees. Merik fell into step next to me. "What do you mean—a gift?"

I looked up at the clouded sky and tried to find the words. It wasn't something that Reynalt or Ryan had ever talked about, but then again, there also weren't many navigators like Seb. "Sebastian has a connection with Kalax. Sometimes he can hear Kalax speak. He's even taught me how to hear Kalax."

I looked over at Varla, expecting her to be rolling her eyes. Instead, she nodded. "It's the Dragon Affinity. About one out of every hundred navigators has it, and even then it might only happen once a generation. I read about it in one of the older books."

Merik nodded as if it was no big deal. "Usually, you hear your dragon's name after months of closely working. Or an older navigator will divine it for you. There are scrolls that talk about protectors and riders waiting years to hear their dragon's name."

I blinked at the two of them. They sounded like this was no big deal—and they believed me.

"The fact that Seb heard your dragon so quickly means he must have the affinity. It's probably why he was so bad to start with, he was always feeling all this stuff from everyone." Varla gave another nod.

We'd reached the tree where their saddles and harnesses hung. I told them to stay put and I climbed up to untangle the straps. Most of them had been broken, but every rider carried spare leather and rope and I was sure we could at least get the saddles repaired.

As I struggled with the harness I thought how impressed Varla had sounded—and Merik—when they were talking about Seb having Dragon Affinity—and how I'd thought so little of him. It was odd to think of him as being more special than anyone—and not just a commoner. He was a lot more than a drunken blacksmith's son. Back on the ground, Merik got busy pulling out spare leather and rope and trying to straighten out the harness. Varla was helping him, but she looked up at me and said, "You should tell Commander Hegarty about Seb. It might help you graduate."

I shook my head. "Not the way that our rankings are going at the moment!" I didn't even want to think about how we were failing right now in the advanced trials. Our flag had probably been captured and we'd show up with no great record of any shots made.

Merik and Varla got their saddles sorted out. They only had a little bit of harness, but it would be enough to get them home—if Ferdinania came back. I helped them carry everything back to the riverbank. I'd just started to think about gathering wood for a fire when Merik pointed to a spot in the sky.

"He's more than good with dragons, I'll say that much," Merik said.

I looked up. The afternoon was fading as the sun drifted low on the horizon. I could see the distinct form of two spots getting larger. Two dragons, one flying much more erratically than the other.

Seb and Kalax were leading Ferdinania. The spots got larger, formed into dragons. Kalax swooped over the trees and landed with a graceful spray on the river. Ferdinania landed too, but on the opposite river bank from us.

Grinning, I didn't wait for Kalax to step out of the river, but splashed over to her and Seb. "You did it!"

Slipping down from his saddle, Seb still looked worried.

He nodded to Merik and Varla, and then to Ferdinania. "She's better. But she's still not feeling the best. She got confused—she thought Ty should be on her, not Merik and what with her not feeling right and that, well, she's sorry now, but she needs some rest. You'll all have to climb onto Kalax for the flight back."

We left Merik and Varla's mended saddles and harness on the riverbank. Someone could come and get them later. Seb helped me into my harness and turned to give Varla and Merik a helping hand. Varla would ride with me, and Merik would ride behind Seb. It would be tight, but we were all light and small.

I saw something unusual sticking out from under our harness, two long, thin rods with golden material wrapped around the end.

Staring at Seb, I asked, "Gold team's flags? From the mountaintop?"

He grinned. "Well, no one was looking out for us—I think they figured Kalax had crashed along with Ferdinania. So, I stopped off on the way back. I thought we might as well finish the challenge." He settled into his saddle, Merik behind him. I stared at Seb, my mouth hanging open.

As we lifted back up into the air, I started to grin. Even if we came last in this challenge, to me it felt like we had achieved more than any other team in the advanced trials. Maybe Seb and I really could be partners. Slowly, my grin faded. I kept thinking that it wasn't any good to have these skills—and be a Dragon Rider—if we didn't put to use what we knew.

Somehow, I had to convince Seb that he and Kalax needed to fly north to see what was really going on up there. But I had no idea how I could change Seb's mind about now wanting to be the perfect cadet who never broke or bent any rules. Varla hung onto me as we flew, and I made up my mind.

If Seb wouldn't come north with me, I'd go on my own.

CHAPTER 23

THE DRAGON ENCLOSURE

The week after the advanced trials, the instructors kept us busy with extra drills and training, and I thought it strange that Thea started taking my side on things a lot more often. Almost as if she was starting to trust me. She let me make the decisions about flying and followed my lead...well, sometimes. She also wasn't hanging out the Beris and Syl as much, but that could be because the instructors were giving us almost too much work. The only ones with any time to spare were Varla and Merik.

Ferdinania was slow to get over her sickness. We all started to worry for her. Commander Hegarty kept Ferdinania on her own, in a special stall at the academy where Varla and Merik could visit her every day. She couldn't fly, and I could tell she didn't like that. But Varla snuck her treats of roast lamb and Merik would sit with her, reading her stories as if she understood every word, and she liked that.

Today was one of our few afternoons off. Commander Hegarty had ordered us some rest now that we were approaching graduation so we had time to study.

Today, Instructor Mordecai also posted a leader board next to the wooden equipment shed. I was the first to see it, and reading down the names I sighed heavily. It was only an indication of whether we would graduate, but it showed what sort of place we might be offered if we made it to the ranks of being a Dragon Rider. Anyone right at the bottom might not even be offered a spot—the instructors could retire the riders' dragon to breeding and the cadets would leave. Or if there was a spot open for courier duties, those riders might be given that task. Riders at the top of the lists might get a spot like Thea's brother Reynalt had and be personal Dragon Riders to the king.

I looked unhappily at the mid-list ranking for Cadet Sebastian Smith and Cadet Agathea Flamma. She had lost a lot of points coming in last in the advanced trials.

Well, we're not at the top, Kalax. I sent a sliver of thought to our red, dimly sensing that she was snoozing in the enclosure in her own cozy cave. It was after lunch and she had feasted on lake fish. I could feel the tight warmth of her belly.

Our bond had grown stronger and it was almost easy to share feelings and thoughts with Kalax. I didn't quite know how much she could sense about me, but it seemed like a lot.

Kalax stirred. Tired. Full. Who cares about lists. I smiled, but it couldn't be further from the truth that no one should care about the list. I cared, and I knew Thea did, too.

Were we still being punished by Mordecai? If Ferdinania hadn't become ill and we had performed well in the advanced trials—and if Mordecai had never caught us—we might be in the top three teams along with Jensen and Wil, and Beris and Syl.

Head down and boots dragging, I headed to the keep. Thea would want to know and I didn't want her to find out by Beris or one of the others being mean about it.

I wondered if we were becoming friends, and real partners. For a moment, a memory flashed of how the fire glowed on her cheeks and the light in her hair as we sat around Arkady's campfire. My stomach did a little flutter.

Why should I feel nervous about seeing Thea? But my mouth went dry anyway and my heart kicked up fast, like in a dive that Kalax was taking. I shook my head to clear it and stepped into the great hall.

Most everyone was grabbing some water or wine or having a rare lunch, since we usually didn't eat much if we had afternoon training. I glanced around, but I didn't see Thea. But Varla sat alone at a table, bent over a book, so I walked over to her. "Have you seen Thea?"

Varla looked up and blinked. "Uh...I think she went off about a half hour ago to get in some extra practice, or so she told me." She shrugged and turned back to her book—a thick one with an old, leather binding.

But we don't have afternoon practice today. I stood staring at great hall, hearing the noise of quiet talk and the scrape of wooden benches on the stone floor.

Why would Thea tell Varla she was going to get in extra practice, and why wouldn't she tell me?

Then it hit me—flying north.

Thea had been desperate to do something about the trouble we'd been hearing about. She'd talked to me every day this past week, trying to convince me that we needed to take a look because no one else would.

Fear gripped my belly. I couldn't let her do this alone, but what if she'd already left? What if she was going by pony? Or what if…?

I cut off the thought. I ran to the stables to catch up with her, but all the mountain ponies were in their stalls, munching on hay or snoozing, one hind-hoof cocked.

Where could she be?

What? Kalax was groggy from sleep, but she was also annoyed. Something had woken her up. I felt something brush Kalax's mind, on the other side of mine—Thea! She was trying to communicate with Kalax as I did, but she was talking to Kalax as if Kalax was only a baby.

What does she want? Kalax's irritation slipped into amusement, and I was glad of that. I didn't want Kalax to be angry with Thea.

Don't worry—it's just that we're going flying, Kalax. I got back a flash of excitement from Kalax.

Returning to the great hall and scribbling a quick note that I handed to Varla, I called out, "Give that to the commander this afternoon, will you?" I didn't wait for an answer but headed for the equipment sheds. I picked up our saddles and harness, glad they were light enough that I could carry them, and headed for the dragon enclosure.

The dragon enclosure sat in the central crater of Mount Hammal. Merik had told me about it, and then had to explain what a volcano was. It was hot like the hottest forge. Natural vents had been widened into caverns and a honeycomb-like system of caves where the dragons slept. At the very bottom, hot springs still bubbled making it humid, green and warm for the dragons.

There were a number of ways to get into the enclosure, most left unguarded because who would want to break into a place guarded by dragons? Still, I tried to be as careful as possible— Dragon Riders or instructors from the academy might be there.

The crater was mostly the playground of the youngest dragons, baby wyrms and hatchlings—any of which could kill you with a bite. The old brood mothers like Heclaxia also spent their days here, lazing on the heated slabs of rock that poked out of the vegetation, fat as well-fed kitchen cats, and just as grumpy.

I tried to send calming thoughts to every dragon around me as I edged the crater and followed a little track up to what I knew was Kalax's cavern.

A hiss had me turning to see an angry-looking green dragon on the rocks above me. She looked a big, brood mother and she stared at a small figure on the inside of the crater. Thea! She stood outside Kalax's cavern, her arms raised as if she was trying to contact Kalax or the big green. I could sense the green brood mother didn't like the intrusion into what she thought of as her space. She wasn't going to back down unless Thea disappeared. Someone else knew this, too.

With a sharp roar, Kalax poured herself out of her cavern, doing her best to both puff out her chest and spit flame into the air.

The brood green backed up a few paces, looking from Kalax to Thea. Kalax was a lot smaller than the green, but a fight between dragons who knew each other well was never something either of them wanted. The brood green seemed to be weighing up the pros and cons of attacking both Thea and Kalax. A long, sonorous, hooting call from the crater floor interrupted—Heclaxia was announcing her dominance.

The brood green huffed out a puff of smoke and stomped back to her cave, making the ground shake.

I rushed over to where Thea stood. She looked pale-faced and shaky. "You shouldn't have done that," I told her. I mentally sent warm thoughts of congratulations to Kalax.

"Seb!" She turned and blinked. "I...I needed to try."

"What? Getting yourself killed? Look, I know you're going to head north. What makes you think I'd let you?" I put myself between her and Kalax's cave.

Her chin lifted. "You don't have to come with me." She glanced at the saddles in my hands. "And I don't have to fly there." She crossed her arms.

Shaking my head, I told her, "I can't let you go on your own. I won't." The feelings that rose in me surprised me. I knew then that it didn't matter what Thea did—she was my partner and I wasn't going to let her get in trouble on her own—not ever.

Head tipped to the side, she seemed to be looking at me in a new way, her eyes a little narrowed but with a look I'd almost call admiring. Without thinking about it, I stepped in and kissed her on the cheek.

I didn't know why I did it, I just knew I had to. I stepped back, unsure of what she was going to say, or if she was going to hit me now.

Next to us, Kalax snorted and a small burst of flame warmed in the air. I turned the same time as Thea and we both laughed.

223

Without saying a word, Thea took one of the saddles from me.

Stomach knotted, I knew we were going to north—and heading into whatever trouble was brewing.

CHAPTER 24

THE MEMORY STONE

I didn't know if it was because of Seb's strange affinity with Kalax, or if it was because of what had happened back at the enclosure, but it felt that we were actually a partnership now, in more ways than one. All of us. Kalax lifted into the air as soft as a feather and flew the best that I had ever known, and Seb and I just seemed to be on the same page for once.

I replayed the feel of his lips against my skin, just a gentle brush, a hint of warmth and softness. It had left me shivering with something like fear, excitement, and butterflies in my stomach all at once. But Dragon Riders were supposed to be partners—not lovers. And as cadets we weren't even supposed to be more than friends. I knew of some Dragon Riders who had eventually settled down and had married—but never while in service. It just…well, it wasn't done.

Thinking ahead, too, I knew that I had to put my duty to the academy and my father and my king first. What if there was a war tomorrow? How could Seb and I fight in battles if we were too…too emotionally entangled? And what would those tangles do to our riding Kalax?

There were too many questions. I almost wished Seb hadn't

kissed me, but I knew deep inside that part of me wished he had done it a lot sooner.

What am I thinking? Father would never agree to an unequal match, and I wanted to be a Dragon Rider, not a woman who would be a wife and mother above all else. My mind was in turmoil and my emotions bounded around like young dragons trying out their wings for the first time. Enough, I thought. For the moment, duty mattered the most. There was a real chance we were all in terrible danger, and I needed to focus on simply finding out if that danger was real or just some stories.

We had to do what was right, meaning we needed to bring back information to the academy if there was a danger forming. We flew high, catching the cold winds. It seemed to me that Kalax enjoyed stretching her wings. The Leviathan Mountains rose in front of us, marching toward us, their peaks as white as linen.

Below us the terrain grew wilder and wilder, the farms breaking up into meadows and ravines, snow-fed streams snaking paths down the foothills. We flew past the occasional shepherd's croft, perched high in the hills, and over deep woods where deer startled and burst into the open, and over lakes that looked ice-cold with blue waters. We had been flying for the best part of the afternoon—Kalax seemed to never tire, and she knew how to ride the thermals to save her strength. Seb and I kept quiet, too, for we needed to save our energy as well. The day was drawing to its close, the sky overhead turning darker, when I saw what we were looking for. A village—and it must be one that had supposedly been taken over by the Darkening. I pointed downward. Seb nodded and coaxed Kalax into a wide circling movement to bring us down.

*   *   *

"Well, it doesn't look as though it's been wiped off the map." I glanced at Seb. We had landed on a wide section of barren land just outside the village, perhaps the place where they might once have held fairs or markets. The simple, two streets of the village all stood before us in as good a condition as you'd expect. A few boards were missing from two of the buildings, a few windows were missing their glass, but the roofs were all intact and not a house was burned to the ground or otherwise demolished. I could see no signs of battle.

Seb was frowning. "But…this village wasn't on any of the maps I saw. And…where is everyone?"

"Look there." I pointed to the surrounding woodlands. A thin wisp of pale smoke rose above the tree line. "Someone has a fire."

"Guess we'd better introduce ourselves," Seb said, drawing his sword from his saddle scabbard. I unslung my bow and notched an arrow, joining him as we crept toward the trees. Kalax moved surprisingly quietly behind us.

The woods surrounding the village seemed unkempt—fallen wood had not been gathered for fires. The trees were tall pines, dry needles crunched under our boots and Kalax's step. Within the forest, we found a narrow track that led to a small, thatched cottage. Lights twinkled from within the clouded windows, and a thin trail of white smoke rose from a stone chimney.

"I'll knock." Seb moved up to the cottage door and raised a fist to rap on the door.

"Hold fast," a voice called from the other side of the clearing. We turned. An old man emerged from the shadows of the trees on the edge of the clearing. He was bald with a long, white beard and he wore dirty brown and tan robes. He held a taut bow in his hand, an arrow notched and aimed at Seb. "Move off, unless you wants a new hole to breathe through." A shadow fell across all of us.

Kalax pushed aside a trio of saplings and rose up in the clearing, her teeth bared and a rumble coming from deep in her chest.

The old man paled and lowered his bow.

Stepping forward, Seb spread his hands wide. "We mean you no harm. We're here…we heard stories. Tales of bad things happening in the north. We came to find out the truth."

"Dragon Riders? From Torvald?" The old man started to

228

shake. Relief eased the lines on his face, but fear still seemed to lurk in his eyes. "I thought you'd never come!"

"Were you attacked?" I asked.

The old man strode forward, glancing over his shoulder, and made for his cottage door. "Come in. You'd best come in." He looked up at Kalax. "Er—there isn't room for all of you, though."

I nodded. Seb put a hand on Kalax's neck. She grumbled, but wrapped herself around the rock of the fireplace and the cottage, warming herself.

Inside, I saw the old man lived simply—a hunter and trapper, I guessed. Skins and furs hung from the rafters, and the place had the smell of preserving vinegars, salts and a musty undercurrent of meat and bone. The old man hung his bow and quiver of arrows on a hook by the side of the door.

He moved to the fire, added a log and gestured for us to sit. His chairs—two of them—looked hand-hewn from logs. I chose to stand near the door. But Seb sat and put his sword across his knees.

The old man glanced from Seb to me and back. He looked tired and weary. He rubbed a hand down his beard. "My grandfather rode the dragons of Torvald, but my father—he was never picked." He glanced at me and his eyes narrowed. "You're a Flamma, aren't you? That hair—like golden fire. My

229

grandfather told me of your line. Said you was cousins, of a kind."

I lifted my eyebrows. I would never claim a man such as this as kin, but I knew the House of Flamma was widespread. "Your story?" I asked, prompting the man.

He shook his head and stared into the fire. "I had gone out to hunt, as I always do, spending a few days in the deep woods, caching what I can't carry, picking up a few rabbits and pheasants, deer and a boar as well. My cart was weighed down by the time I returned to the village. I came by the old path, the one up to the mines. And what I seen—well, it weren't right. Men, women, children all—everyone staggering in and out of the old mine like they was asleep but with their eyes open. But they weren't carrying ore out—all the ore from the old mine was used up years ago. They were just carrying rocks."

"Big rocks?" I asked.

The old man scratched his beard and shook his head. "All sizes. I couldn't understand it. I tried asking a few what they were doing—old Tom the butcher, and Ralph the smithy. Wouldn't say a word. Wouldn't even stop for me. Mindless, they were. Just walking in and out of the mine, carrying rocks. Next thing, I hear hoof beats a-coming. I hide by picking up a rock and being one of those without a mind. And up comes a black rider on a black horse. In one hand, he's toying with something hung around his neck. A green stone…a jewel the size of your fist…and I stare into it and feel my past leaking away."

"The Memory Stone," Seb breathed out the words. I hushed him and turned back to the old man. "What happened next?"

He let out a breath, looked up at us and leaned back in his chair. "House of Flamma. Grandda always said House of Flamma made the best riders. Said his own gran came from that house. Ran off she did, to her family's disapproval."

My patience was wearing, but Seb leaned forward and said, "What of you? Can you remember?"

The old man shook his head. "I wakes in a camp full of the sleepers. Don't know why I wakes and they don't. I got up and ran back to the village, but the people didn't run with me. Under a spell, I figure. A wicked magic. Just like in the old tales."

I crossed my arms. "If there is magic, why didn't you stay under the spell?"

Seb glanced at me. "Maybe the magic doesn't work on everyone the same." He looked at the old man. "What do you think is different about you?"

Shrugging, the old man looked at me. "Maybe it's cause I've Dragon Riders' blood in me. It's weak and old as me, but it's there. Or maybe it's 'cause I didn't look long enough into that stone. Maybe that black rider couldn't steal all my soul."

231

Frowning, I tried to will Seb not to keep asking questions. It was possible this old man was just mad from living too many years on his own. He might be spinning stories, too—maybe he was even the one who had started the stories of trouble. There could be a lot of reasons for the village to be empty—maybe a sickness had started and spread, or those who lived here had left to follow rumors of gold. But I knew that even if those things were true, a few should still be here. And not just this old man.

"You know what's going on, don't you?" the old man asked, his voice anxious. "The Darkening—it's returning. That black rider with his black eyes is bringing it back."

Stepping over to him, I put a hand on his shoulder. "Make your way to Torvald, get yourself behind strong city walls and close to the city."

Seb stood. "Thea's right. This...this looks as if the Darkening is returning—and if that old evil has the power of magic with it, no one is safe. We must get back to the academy and warn others."

I sent Seb a worried glance. We didn't have any real proof—just an empty village that was not on any map and an old man with more stories to tell. But still, it might be enough to set up an alarm. I turned to the old man. "Get yourself to Torvald. You'll be safe there."

He spread his hands wide. "But my cottage? My wife is buried outside."

"You want to be buried next to her?" Seb asked.

The old man shook his head. With a sigh, he nodded. "I'll pack and set out in the morning."

Seb headed outside and I followed. The air was colder now, and the darkness thick. I couldn't help but look around us and wonder where the black rider was—and what his plans were. There was trouble in the land—and now we had to sound the alarm before it was too late to halt its spread.

CHAPTER 25

THE ATTACK

We headed back to the open area near the village; Thea, me and Kalax. I needed time to think about what the old man had said. Why hadn't he stayed under the power of the stones? Could some resist it? Or was there a limit to the stones' power? Or had he been let go for a reason? His stories worried me. Thea mounted into the protector's saddle behind me. Kalax nudged me with her nose. We go home?

I could tell she was tired. She needed rest, as did I. With a nod to Thea, I mounted and asked Kalax to fly south. We flew through the early hours of the evening and into the night. I was surprised at how quickly she responded to my mental commands. She'd taken to night flying almost immediately. I could tell she liked the cool air on her face and the stars glittered overhead. The cold wind, however, seeped through my leather jerkin and now I wished I'd worn a warmer, winter cloak.

Finally, the pale towers of the Dragon Academy rose up. We could see them from behind the ridge of Mount Hammal. But I also saw the beacon torches blazing from the tops of the walls. Something was very wrong—the beacons were only lit in times of great danger. Or war.

In the distance the Dragon Horn sounded three long calls. Kalax stiffened underneath me and picked up speed. Three blasts was a summons to all riders to arm and mount.

We circled our platform and descended to see one of the Dragon Riders waving landing flags at us, telling us to land and dismount immediately. Down in the training area and also on top of the walls, Dragon Riders ran, hastily pulling on their armor and grabbing their saddles, weapons and harness. Overhead, dragons swept from the sky, landing on platforms, giving out small bursts of fire that lit the night. Along with the beacon torches, the dragon fire left the air smelling of smoke and the night seemed to take on a reddish haze.

I swapped a look with Thea—she glanced at me, her mouth tight and her eyes huge. Thea gave Kalax a pat. "She should get some food and rest."

I nodded. We quickly unsaddled Kalax, and I told her to go back to her cave to eat and rest. She looked at me. No flying? Want to fly!

Eat first, I told her.

She puffed out smoke and took off. Heading down into the training yard with our saddle and harness, I saw a small knot of people in front of the keep. Commander Hegarty stood out in full battle array.

He glanced at us and smiled. "Sebastian. Agathea. Thank the heavens you are safe. We thought you been caught up in the attack."

Panic knotted my stomach. "What attack? What's happened?"

The commander put a hand on my shoulder. "Enemy dragons…black dragons have been spotted, coming from the north. We've had word of two villages having been attacked, and that an army of mindless slaves marches with black dragons. We're preparing for war."

"The Darkening," I muttered. It was coming at us, sooner than I thought it would. Next to me, Thea pulled in a sharp breath.

Commander Hegarty was looking grave. He turned and ordered those around to head to their dragons.

"Sir, we're ready to ride," Thea said stepping forward.

The commander shook his head. "You and the other cadets are to stay here at the academy. Your job is to keep it secured. The Dragon Riders will deal with this threat."

"But Commander…" The words poured out of me. I had left the commander a note saying that Thea and I were practicing night flight—that way at least I'd known we'd come back and not get a third mark against us. But no one was thinking of marks now. I told him about the stones, the mines, the empty village we'd found, and about the old man's story. The commander's mouth pulled down and his eyes sharpened. "Sir, we think the Darkening is returning."

Next to me, Thea nodded. "It's true, sir. The stories from the north—and the story about a…a stone that can steal memories."

Hegarty looked from Thea to me. "The Memory Stone—that is something you should not mention again. Not to others. There is too much danger in the knowledge of that stone. We'll speak more later. For now, you have your orders." Commander Hegarty clapped a heavy, firm hand on my shoulder and one on Thea's. "Your time will come, cadets. By the First Dragon, it may be more quickly than you think." He turned and strode away, heading up the stairs to the platform where his dragons waited.

I turned to Thea. I felt helpless, and worried. Did these riders even know the danger they faced? Could they win against magic? The old stories said they'd had the dragon stones with them— what would happen if those stones were in the hands of the Darkening? Shoulders slumping, I nudged her with my elbow. "I guess we have our orders now."

Thea was looking up at the dark bodies of the winged dragons flying hard against the rising wind, circling over the academy as they formed into squadrons and rank. Turning to me with fire in her eyes, Thea shook her head. "I know this is going to mean disobeying the commander—something that will get us both kicked out. But we have to choose—stay and maybe there would

237

be an academy that will take us in as full Dragon Riders, or kick us out. Or ride to save our city and the realm."

I shook my head. "The commander knows what he's up against. We told him—that's what we wanted to do." Thea punched my arm. Hard. Pulling back I glared at her. "What was that for?"

"This is the most important thing that's ever happened in my life. Ever! Do you really want to stay here and wait? We might be cadets, but what if the commander needs to send messages? What if the Darkening, whatever it is, is stronger than even the king's Dragon Riders? You have skills no one else has, Seb. You heard what the old man said—there's magic at work. Dark magic. And what the commander said—black dragons on the move. There are cadets enough to hold the academy—but they're going to be dead, too, if whatever is moving against us defeats the Dragon Riders. And if there's one thing I've learned it's that one person can make a difference. Now are we going? Or are we going to let everyone down?"

I let out a breath. As long as I had Thea and Kalax by my side, I wouldn't ever hesitate again.

"Let's go. But I want a heavier cloak first. And if we're going to ride with Dragon Riders, we'd better look like them, too. So whose helmets and armor do you think we can borrow?"

With all the rushing around and confusion, it was fairly easy to fill saddle bags with food from the kitchen and grab extra armor and weapons from the sheds. I asked Kalax if she had eaten, and she had, but she wanted to be up in the air. She had caught the excitement of the other dragons and didn't want to miss this. She was just like Thea. I kept worrying, but Thea's eyes sparkled bright in the torchlight as if she lived for this kind of thing. I tried not to think about getting caught—there were more important worries, like ones about staying alive.

Once saddled, Kalax followed the rest of the Dragon Riders. We flew north, hanging back behind the last flight squadron. We had been about two hours in the saddle when I noticed Kalax was starting to tire. Her wings dipped lower each time she beat them and her long neck wavered as she tried to hold up her head.

Ahead of us, the experienced dragons knew how to use the air currents that flowed over the ridgelines of hills, ducking low over lakes and rivers, saving their energy. The experienced Dragon Riders knew how to pace themselves—and they hadn't already made this flight north, unlike us.

We almost lost the squadron twice as the dragons flew low over the forests and woods below, never daring to raise themselves up high in the sky, which would give away their position to any enemy watchers.

But where was the enemy? I scanned the horizon. There was no glow of fire, no smoke, no terrible sounds of battle. It was as if we were just flying a night training mission. The dragon squadron changed their pace, rising in the air in vast swooping movements. I realized we were nearing the village that must have reported that they were under attack.

"There," Thea leaned forward to point out to a spot ahead of us. Nestled against a low hill, I glimpsed the glow of camp fires dotting the woods. I gasped when I realized the size of the camp—there had to be thousands of Dragon Riders spread over the edge of the woods and the river.

"But where's the village they're here to protect?" Thea asked as I used one of my telescopes to scan the dark horizon, but everything was too black to make anything out. Finally, I spotted a dark collection of irregular shapes. The village was actually a walled town, with high walls rising on one side of a river and the bluff of hills behind. Two bridges spanned the river. Inside the walled township, I could see not a hint of light.

I shivered. It was just like the other village we had seen earlier—deserted.

I turned to ask Thea where we should land, when a pain shot through the side of my head. It was as if a blazing poker had been pushed into my skull.

"Seb!" Thea shouted, and then Kalax roared. I swayed and started to fall from my saddle. Too many wings, too many …

Thea grabbed my shoulder and shook me. Underneath me, Kalax wobbled and dove—I knew she could feel my pain and it was unbearable. I cried out and Kalax roared again and dove, trying to escape my own confusion and agony.

"Land us," Thea yelled.

I managed to get the picture of what I wanted to do to Kalax. She skimmed over the edge of the woods beyond the king's camp, landing awkwardly with a disgruntled squawk in a small clearing.

Thea unclipped me from my harness and dragged me to the ground. Above us, Kalax hissed into the air. "What is it?" Thea demanded.

"Too many...too many dragons. I can feel them..." The pain began to ease to a low and steady thump behind my eyes.

"Your Dragon Affinity. Looks like there are drawbacks to your gift." Thea sat back on her heels. Under me, the ground was cool and steadied me. Thea glanced over to the fires on the hillside. "Something's made it worse. But you never had this trouble at the academy, and we have a lot of dragons there. Maybe it's their excitement, or maybe it's the Dragon Egg Stones..."

I sat up. I didn't know why it had hit me like that, either. I could feel the waves of fear and excitement coming from all of the dragons. Some dragon minds were sharper and more distinct—I knew which dragons I met at the academy. But somewhere nearby, there was also a tide of hunger and anger. I had the feeling these were the black dragons that the Dragon Riders would be facing.

"You'll have to rest," Thea said, one hand on my chest. Kalax gave a welcoming chirrup and sat down heavily beside me. She folded one of her wings around me and Thea. It was like being surrounded by her heartbeat. The pain eased and I closed my eyes, but still I could feel the threat of the black dragons.

CHAPTER 26

THE MINES

Kalax curled protectively around Seb. She didn't look as though she was going to budge at any time soon—her eyes closed along with Seb's. I was up when Kalax had moved and had stepped away. Now, I stared at the two of them, worried. Seb was white—I could see that even in the dim moonlight. Sweat plastered his brow.

He had never had a problem when he lived right next to the dragon enclosure, but we didn't have this many dragons at the academy. And then again, a lot of things had happened in the last couple of days—magical stones seemed to be emerging out of the past and mythical enemies were turning up from nowhere.

I was hoping Seb's skill might actually prove to be of some value if we ended up fighting the black dragons. But it wouldn't be any help if it left Seb like this. Could he learn to control it and not let it overwhelm him like this?

From far off I could hear snatches of voices coming from the nearest part of the Dragon Rider camp. We had landed a short distance away and I could smell the food cooking on their fires.

I nodded, as much to myself as to Kalax, who opened one eye halfway. I felt stupid, but I said, "Kalax, I'm going into camp to find out what the situation is. I'll be back soon."

Kalax breathed a deep, rasping chirrup in the back of her throat. I had no idea if that meant she understood me or just that she was going to go to sleep. I knew we all needed rest—we'd flown north twice this day and my legs, arms and back ached. I could wish myself back in bed, but I was not leaving this to others. We were stepping into legend. Nodding to myself, I adjusted my bow and set off for the nearest campfire.

The Dragon Riders were camped in the traditional groupings, with each squadron circled around a fire. It was easy to spot the banners fluttering over the fires, but I wanted to work out a way into the nearest camp without being questioned by any guards.

The last thing I wanted to do was to get shot by my own side. I skirted the edge of the camp and found an overly sleepy guard, leaning against a sleeping dragon. I strode past him, keeping my steps light and quick.

The camp had one main fire burning in the center of the circle of dragons. Beside this, tents had been put up and smaller cooking fires lit. A pot of meat sat over one fire, and my stomach growled. I'd missed dinner. The camps were all far enough from roads or open spaces that the trees would provide some protection. Glancing around, I could see flickering lights glimmering through the trees, each campfire spaced twenty or thirty meters apart, stretching as far as the eye could see.

244

The Dragon Riders hadn't been deployed like this—in full force—for decades. Ever since the academy had been formed, Torvald had only engaged in a few minor skirmishes. Often as not, the Dragon Riders went after pirates and a few marauding vagabonds from the wilderness.

I walked through the camp, my head lowered so my borrowed Dragon Rider armor and horned helmet would hide my face. I pulled my cloak firmly around me.

"Hey," a harsh male voice called out.

Oh, dragon crap! I turned so it would look like I had stopped to listen to him, but I kept my face down. There weren't any women in the Dragon Riders that I knew of just now. If anyone saw my face, or my hair, they'd figure out right away who I was and that I was still a cadet.

"You Dragon Riders gonna do something about them over there?" I glanced over and saw one of the foot soldiers who made up the ground army. He must have been stationed nearby in order to get here as quickly as the Dragon Riders—perhaps he had even been with those who had called for help.

I nodded, not saying anything.

"Well, you'd better hurry up about it. Go back and tell the rest of your lot to get on with it."

I nodded again, turned and hurried off in the opposite

direction.

I headed into the next camp. This one had the bigger command tents set up. This was where Commander Hegarty would be. A rising sense of panic lifted in my chest. He would see through my disguise with ease—he knew all the cadets too well. But then I saw something that made my heart swell—the flame of House Flamma emblazoned on a banner hung before one of the big tents. That had to be Reynalt's tent. As head of a squadron, he would be near the command tents. I split off from the main track, pulled the tent flap aside and ducked in.

My shoulders eased down. With a vast sense of relief, I saw the tent was empty. I had planned to plead with him to take us on in his squadron, but this was far better. His tent was large, with sleeping rugs, a folding table, and a weapons rack. I edged over to the table. Maps and scrolls of paper littered it. Red lines indicated options for attack and defense, but a strange sigil, like an X, stood out on the map. The mark indicated a spot further up the bluff along the river cliffs, a distance away from the village.

I'd seen that mark before—Seb had talked to me about it when we'd been training and going over map marks. He'd called it a mark for a mine, and had told me the circle around the mark was for a mine that produced the ore needed to make Dragon Rider armor.

Staring at the map, I suddenly knew what all this meant. It was as if everything suddenly fit—the commander's warning that even knowing about the stones was a danger, the gypsy stories about the stones being used, but how no one now seemed to know about them. The villages vanishing—Seb's talk about maps and mines and danger. It all made sense to me.

The stones must have been hidden—long, long ago. They were thought a danger, and so they'd been put away and had become a secret. And now…now the Darkening was looking for them. Which meant this attack on the villages was a distraction. The real aim had to be the mines—that's where I would have hidden the stones: with more stones, where the magical ones would be hard to find. And that was why the old man had talked about the people of his village being made to move rocks—they'd been looking for more of the powerful stones.

I sucked in a breath. Hadn't the story been that there was one special Dragon Stone that could control everything—or let one person use all the stones at once? Was that what the Darkening wanted? With it, could it destroy all Dragon Riders?

Stepping forward, I took up a quill out of the red-ink pot and drew a large circle around the mine. I also drew in the word, Darkening. Reynalt would notice the change in the map and at least want to know what was up—he was even more curious than I.

Grabbing a flagon of wine and one of water, I headed back to

Seb and Kalax.

CHAPTER 27

THE DARKENING

"Seb…Seb, you have to wake." A hand shook my shoulder. I blinked my eyes open. Faint sunlight flashed in my eyes, as well as moisture off the slightly damp snout of Kalax. I spluttered, coughed and realized I had been asleep for most of the night. The pale dawn warmed the eastern sky and the stars were winking out.

"Huh? It's okay. What's happened?" I reached up to pat Kalax's horned snout, reassuring her that I was indeed alive and well, and that yes, I was getting up now. My muscles had stiffened from sleeping on hard ground, but the warm belly of our dragon felt good against my back.

Thea sat down close to me and offered a skin of water. I drank it back. I had vague, painful memories of last night—of collapsing in the woods, of my mind confusing Kalax, of nearly crashing.

A snort from Kalax had me turning to look at her. She thought it was funny how I thought I could control her every move. I landed fine, she thought at me. "Oh, right," I told her.

"Right what?" Thea asked. She looked at me, eyes narrowed. "You're not still funny in the head are you?"

I rubbed my forehead. "The headache…it's almost gone now, just in the very back of my mind." Beyond Kalax, I could hear the dull murmur of other dragon's minds, like the buzz of distant rain. It was just like at the academy now. "I…I don't know what happened. It was like something kind of sharpened my Dragon Affinity somehow. I don't really understand it," I said, reaching out to pat Kalax's hide reassuringly.

Thea stood and started pacing in front of me. "I need to tell you a few things." Hands waving wildly, she told me about what she had discovered in camp—the map and its marks—and what she suspected.

"We have to tell the commander," I said, staggering to my feet.

Thea shook her head. "Do you know how long that will take—assuming we can even get close to the commander? Look." She pointed to the camps. I could see dragons stirring, lifting into the air to go hunt breakfast before they were saddled. "The camps are going to be full of riders—and everyone's going to want to know who we are, why we're here, and my bet is they'll stuff us into a tent to wait for punishment."

I glanced at Thea. "For disobeying orders. We're not supposed to be here."

Thea nodded. "Maybe we can make that work for us. And I think I know why your affinity with dragons suddenly went off the scale—what if that means the Dragon Stone is here?"

Shaking my head, I told her, "We're taking a huge risk."

She nodded. "Yes, we are. But isn't that what Dragon Riders are supposed to do. Now, here's what I had in mind." Squatting down, she started to draw in the dirt with a stick.

*   *   *

Within the hour we were flying over the trees, keeping the river on our left as we sped up the valley. Looking behind us, I could see a cloud of dragons like seagulls, circling, landing and slowly ascending into the air over the camp. The Dragon Riders were amassing and maybe the battle would start today.

Spookily, there was no sign or action from the town, but I sensed a dark menace coming from within the walls. I looked away.

The mine was further than Thea had thought from looking at the map. It was well toward afternoon when we spotted the pronounced holes and stone pillars that marked the mines.

"There," I said and asked Kalax to land near the river and the base of the cliff.

A roar, loaded with intense anger, filled my ears. Pain flashed into me, cutting off all thought. A savage hunger filled me, leaving me dizzy and sick.

"Seb!" Thea shouted.

I glanced back to see her holding onto the saddle with one hand while she reached for her bow with the other. A black shape flashed past us then rose to blot out the sun. I could feel its hatred like a blow, falling onto us. Kalax roared in distress. Looking up, I saw a black dragon, much larger than Kalax and probably bigger than Heclaxia even. It fanned out its wings, hovering for a moment before it dove toward us.

I had no doubt who it was—one black rider sat on the dragon's back. I shivered and knew this had to be the leader of the Darkening. I threw Kalax into a dive, barely meters away from the black dragon's outstretched claws. Wisps of smoke rose from the behemoth's jaws.

From behind me, I heard the twang of Thea's arrows being released. I saw her arrow bounce off the dragon's armored scales. Her shots would do no good on it unless she managed to hit it in the eye.

The black was gaining on us. It was as fast as Kalax and so much bigger that it was clear that she was no match. My head hurt again, the headache growing until it wrapped around my temples and I wanted to rip off my helmet.

"More coming! East and west!" Thea shouted, aiming at the smaller, black dragons rising from the river.

How can we fight off a horde of dragons? I thought. I decided we could only do what we knew how to best.

We would fly.

Kalax responded to my commands, winnowing down close to the river, then rolling over the canopy of the trees, zig-zagging, changing this way and that in mid-air. Her wings stretched out as rigid as they could go, holding for a second then flicking. The big black dragon was gaining, and I could feel pain and madness in his mind—he might have once been a kind dragon, but something had made him into a beast who thought only of killing. There was only one thing left to do—Kalax would be faster with just me on her, and on the ground Thea might escape.

"Seb? What? Wait," Thea was shouting. Trees rushed past us, leaves exploding around us. "You have to jump," I shouted back at her. Two of the smaller black dragons tried to cut us off. Kalax rolled and turned. "Thea, Kalax is faster with only one human on board. And…and you might even be able to shoot the dragons from the ground." I knew she had to think she was doing this to help Kalax and me or she'd never leave us.

It took Thea a moment to slip out of her harness. She grabbed her bow and her quiver of arrows. I could only guess how terrified she must be with the ground a blur as it rushed past us.

Stay alive. I didn't say it, but thought the words at her. Kalax turned, and Thea tumbled into the trees. I glanced back to see her rolling up to her feet and run for the deeper woods.

Now you. Me. Stay alive. Kalax's worry broke into my mind.

Yes, I thought. We need to. Asking her to head up into the sky, I was determined to lose our pursuers so we could come back and rescue Thea. But first we had to stay alive—and the black dragons were closing on us again.

CHAPTER 28

DRAGON EGG STONES

I was angry with Seb. He wouldn't be able to defend himself without a protector. But he wasn't wrong. Kalax would be faster if it was just Seb on her back. But how could he out-fly them all? My shoulders ached from hitting a tree branch. I'd scraped my cheek, but I'd kept myself loose, just the way I had been taught at the academy for when falling off a dragon. I'd never thought I'd have to use that skill.

I could hear screeching cries overhead, but I was far under the cover of thick, tall trees. I'd lost my bow in the fall and without it my arrows weren't much use. I did have a sword in a scabbard at my side—it had banged against me as I fell. But bruises didn't matter. I jogged through the forest, following the keening of the enemy dragons. The tree cover faded as the sound of the dragons grew more distant. Stepping out of the forest, I saw the dragons—the blacks and our red—had dwindled to mere specks in the clouds.

I was alone. Far from the camp or anyone's help.

How could I find my way back? Or should I wait for Seb—but what if he didn't return? My mind swirled around and around, dark thoughts of being lost, of being overrun by black dragons or enemy warriors filled me. For the first time in what seemed like my entire life, I had no one to stand by my side—not my family, not my fellow cadets, and not even Seb.

A chill wind swept down from the north, rattling the leaves in the trees and making me aware of just how ill-equipped I really was to be out here on my own. I could hear the river not far from me and I started in that direction. At least the river would keep me from getting lost. The forest didn't really make any sense to me. I was no navigator, and I hadn't studied the different types of tree, or rocks or how to make emergency shelters. I was in enemy territory.

Searching for my bow I thought how always someone had been with me. My strong brothers or my father, and even Seb had been there for me. I'd taken them all for granted.

My family's expectations had felt like a prison, but now I realized it was in fact a safety-net. What am I doing, thinking I can retrieve the Dragon Egg Stones? "Maybe I am just a foolish child," I said, hearing the echo of my father's words on the wind.

No.

Despite my aches, I straightened. I wasn't a child. I wasn't foolish. I wore the armor of a Dragon Rider and I was a Flamma. I would not fail as a Dragon Rider, and would not fail my family, my city, or my king.

Gritting my teeth, I knew I had to keep going. Searching, I found my bow. It wasn't broken, and I took that as a good omen.

Now, I needed to get back into the sky. Seb had told me I could shoot from the ground, but both of us forgot to figure in that the black dragons would fly off after him. Well, it was time he came back, and that was that. So, how did I get Kalax and Seb back?

I tried to remember the feeling of how I had connected with the dragon. We had touched minds once, and since I was Seb's partner, if anyone could share that affinity with Kalax, it would be me. She had chosen me, too. Closing my eyes, I tried to remember the feeling of the wind through my hair, the warm pulse of Kalax's heartbeat steady through my body. A sense of peace descended on me. I could almost feel the lurch in my stomach as gravity dropped away—

Thea?

My name was as loud in my mind as if someone standing beside me had said it. I knew it was Kalax. I could feel her joy at hearing from me.

Kalax, I need help—I'm near the river.

Wait. Kalax and Seb come for you. I could sense her, weaving through cliffs and caverns—she was losing the last of the black dragons that had been after her. She wheeled and started back to me, and I caught a hint of an argument between her and Seb—how danger was still close.

Which is why you need me, I told Kalax.

It seemed to take forever before her shadow fell over the

rocky banks of the river. I looked up and stepped from the woods where I'd been hiding. The day was growing long and the sun was already nearing the horizon by the time I remounted and we were on our way to the mines in the river's cliff.

I thumped Seb on the back of his head, my hand clanking on his helmet. "Don't ever dump me like that again."

He glanced back at me. "It worked."

I looked around. I didn't like that the black dragons were gone—did that mean they'd headed off to fight the Dragon Riders? My brothers would be in the middle of that fight. But I couldn't worry about that right now. The cliffs were rising in front of us.

Kalax landed on a sandy ledge in front of the main mine workings. Tall pillars of stone rose up around a dark hold. The entrance was too small for her to fit. Seb took some time with her, quietly communing with Kalax and reassuring her that we would be well. I wasn't entirely sure that was going to be the case, but I smiled at Kalax just the same. I could tell she didn't believe us because she made a low, threatening grumble in the back of her throat. She took herself over to a tall outcropping of reddish rock that perfectly disguised her and settled down to keep watch.

I caught a warning to be careful from Kalax, and then Seb turned to me, his eyes wide and dark with either fear or excitement, or maybe both. "You ready?" he asked, pulling out his sword.

"I am," I said and hefted the sword in my hand. Which, in a weird way, I realized I did actually feel ready. Not in the sense that I was prepared to beat every opponent, but I was going to go inside this mine, and I was going to do my best to put a stop to the terror that was besieging the realm. I'd left my bow and arrows on my saddle—they wouldn't be much good inside the narrow tunnels of the mine.

We stepped inside. The main shaft seemed huge, but as we walked, it narrowed. Light from the outside drifted in for a ways, but the farther we went, the darker it got. Soon, we had to edge forward with one hand on the smooth side of the wall to feel our way. The mine smelled like damp rock and something vaguely salt-like. The ground underfoot was smooth, and I could hear the trickle and drip of water seeping in.

Near the entrance I'd seen braces of iron or old timbers to hold up the walls and ceiling. Terrible thoughts of what would happen if the supports gave way filled my mind until I bit my lip so the pain would make me focus. The mine wasn't that cold, but my face still felt chilled and I was glad of my cloak and armor. And then we came to a tunnel that was lit by a torch and which branched off in two different directions.

"Which way?" I said, instinctively turning to my navigator.

Seb paused, cocked his head and then sniffed, breathing out

through his mouth.

"What are you doing?" I hissed at him.

"Something we were taught in navigator lessons. When blinded, you can use your mouth and nose to detect scents on the air." He did it again, beside each opening, then pulled a face. "Hmm. Something fresher this way, like clean water," he nodded in one direction. "But this direction. There's something bitter. Like burning ash. "

"You sure you're not smelling these torches?"

He glanced at me. "They smell like wood smoke." He took the lead, heading toward the bitter smell.

Fire would mean people, which also could mean enemies.

We stepped back into dark tunnels. The ground changed from smooth surface into a rocky surface and we had to watch our step. Whomever had dug out this section of the tunnels must have been in a hurry, since they had not been properly finished. The place had a feel of age to it—and something else. Something that left my skin tingling.

I caught a faint worry from Kalax and then Seb caught my wrist to halt me and whispered, "I hear something."

I froze. I didn't even want to breathe lest I give our position away. I could hear my heart thumping in my chest, so loud I thought everyone must be able to hear it. Seb crouched low, and

260

then I heard what he had.

The sound of booted feet coming closer.

A circle of radiance started to grow larger. My heart thumped harder. The smell of burning wood grew stronger along with another, bitter smell. I could hear only one set of boots approaching. I could handle that. I tugged on Seb's sleeve, and then pushed him back, up against the tunnel wall.

The light brightened. I held up a warning hand to Seb, and then a figure appeared before us. I stuck out my leg in a sweep-kick, connecting with the side of the man's knee in a sickening crack. He fell to the floor with a loud thump. Before he could move, I lifted my sword and hit him on the head with the hilt.

Breathing hard, I straightened.

"Thea, I think you've killed him," Seb hissed at me. I glanced at the man on the tunnel floor.

A wave of nausea lifted in my stomach. Is this what it is like to kill someone? This quick? But the man wasn't dead. I saw his chest lift and fall with breath. He didn't look like a Dragon Rider, or even a foot soldier in the king's army. He wore studded, black leather breeches, heavy black boots, and a mix of hide and leather vests, tied to each other. His long, fair hair was tied into two braids, and he looked a lot bigger than either of my brothers.

"He's a Wildman," Seb said.

I gave a snort. Wildmen was a term used for any of the roaming tribes that occupied the mountains and beyond. They moved with the seasons, fighting each other and against others. They raided more than they traded, and I wondered why such a man would be here. Then I thought of the black dragons.

"Seb, black dragons are wild dragons. Untamable. But someone was riding them. Do you think the Darkening found a way to make them do its bidding—with the stones? Is it doing the same to the Wildmen as well as to villagers?

Seb glanced at me. The torch the Wildman had been carrying cast shadows over Seb's face. "An alliance of the enemies of King Durance? That would be bad. But it would explain why I feel—the black dragons all seem to be in pain. They're half mad with it."

I swallowed. Seb looked at me and nodded down the tunnel. "This way. We should keep going."

The light dwindled as we left the glimmer of the unconscious guard's torch. I gave a thought to picking it up, but if we carried it with us, anyone else down here would also be able to see our approach, just as we had seen the guard's. We were better off without it. Seb led us deeper into the mine. I didn't know what senses he was following, but he was certain. Several times I saw him stop and put a hand to his head, as if something was pounding at him. I put a hand on his shoulder, but he just touched my fingers with his and then moved on.

The walls around us grew slick with some type of moss. It didn't make sense to me that something could be living down here, so far from the light—and then I saw there was light. In the rock, wandering veins of something that gave off a very gentle light. Stepping closer, I could see the rocks glowed with a faint, bluish-white haze.

"Catch-crystals," Seb whispered to me. "We were told about them in navigator class. They're rare. They can catch light, sound and energy, and return it as this glow."

I looked at my friend, his face bathed in an ethereal blue, and thought he looked like a ghost. I hoped we weren't about to become that.

We trudged on. We weren't in the main mine anymore. I could see that from how the walls changed from straight, carved and held up by wood, and shifted into raw caves. This didn't look like it was fashioned by any human hand. Every now and again, I saw something like a whorl or a circle on the rock that looked as if it might be an ancient carving.

Seb stepped out into a wider cavern and put a hand out to halt me next to him. The floor looked to be of soft, silver-grey sand that caught the light of the crystals. The walls were smoothed into ripples of rock. It looked as though water had flowed through here for a long time, years and years ago. The whole place was veined with the lines of catch-crystals, giving the room an eerie glow.

Pointing at the walls, Seb nudged me with his other hand. Between the glowing crystals, I glimpsed designs carved into the rock. Deep stone-cut ridges of lines and circles, unmistakably made by human artisans. One design, curved into whorls and circles, was certainly a dragon. Seb gestured to the other side of the cavern, where a storm of the whirling, carved dragons played across the walls. Some looked like long-necked blues, others were squat greens, and some were long-tailed reds like Kalax.

"But what is that?" Seb whispered.

I turned and looked. The drawings all seemed to converge or point to a design on the largest wall of the chamber. It showed three, rounded egg shapes. Above them, a larger egg shape gave off rays that fell down on the other three shapes.

"The stones—and the one that controls them all," Seb whispered with wonder in his voice.

Across from us, I spotted a narrow tunnel. The sound of gentle hissing came from it. I lifted my sword and whispered, "Dragon?"

Seb shook his head. "Underground water." He stepped across the sand and headed toward the tunnel. I followed. The hissing grew louder to a rush. The catch-crystals around us flared brighter, almost as if they knew we were here, or were reacting to our movement.

Stopping again, Seb pointed. Ahead of us, I could see the

yellowish burn of torchlight and I could hear voices.

Seb eased forward. I came after him, my sword slick in my sweating hand. We stepped into the narrow tunnel, but it widened again out into another cavern. Instead of the floor being covered with sand, this one had a pool of water that stretched over half the cavern floor. Yellow torches cast fitful light over the stale water and illuminated two men who faced each other.

They stood before oddly-shaped pillars of stones that rose from the cavern floor. One man looked a broad-shouldered warrior, clad in mail, with leather binders and a black, fur cloak. He held a heavy mace in one hand. Around him lay strewn rocks, and his face gleamed with sweat as if he'd been pounding at the stone. He looked as big as my brother, Reynalt, but with his scarred face, I would wager he was far meaner.

The second figure, though, worried me more. Long, dark hair was held back with a strand of silver, such as the kings of old might wear. He dressed in black, with studded gauntlets, and I caught of flash of something from his chest—a jewel of some kind, I guessed. His pale, narrow face twisted with anger. "It's not here."

His voice sent shivers down my spine. It was somehow cold, icy as a storm in the depths of winter. For an instant, I felt almost compelled to step forward. Next to me, Seb shifted. I put a hand on him to keep him put.

The older warrior glanced at the man in black. "It has to be. The scroll said the mine of old, and this is the oldest known."

These men had to be here searching for the Dragon Egg Stones, but from the sound of it, they hadn't found them. Next to me, Seb shifted and made as if to rise. I put a hand on him and he stilled again.

"Lord Vincent, I've searched everywhere. That cursed scholar lied to us before he died."

Lord Vincent turned to the warrior. "Wulfric, should I take your head now for your failure?" Wulfric bowed his head, his face pale in the flickering torchlight.

Who was this Lord Vincent that he had so much power that he could terrify an obviously capable warrior?

"I will stay and search for the second stone again," Wulfric said.

I tugged on Seb's sleeve. It was time for us to leave. But Seb eyes had glazed. He stared at Lord Vincent—no, at the jewel Lord Vincent wore—as if he could not look away. He slipped from my hold and stood, his boot knocking a chunk of loose rock that clattered away.

With a swirl of his black cloak, Lord Vincent turned and barked, "Who goes there."

Again, I felt compelled to step forward. But then green

flashed from the jewel Lord Vincent wore. I looked away from that gem—if this was the same one the old man in the woods had run into, it could make me mindless. And was it already working on Seb? I needed a distraction, and something to shake Seb from his seeming trance, so I stood and shouted, "In the name of Torvald, you are wanted for crimes against the innocent, acts of war against the rightful king. In the king's name, I bid you to come peacefully."

Lord Vincent stiffened and his lips curved in a faint smile "What is this? Who sends children after me?" He fingered the jewel on his chest.

I stared at his boots and kept my blade in front of me. "I am Agathea of the House Flamma and I bid you yield."

Lord Vincent laughed. "It would almost be a shame to dirty my blade on you, but what are two more casualties in what will be an all too short war?" He drew his long sword in a smooth flourish.

I tried to bluff, to buy us time until I thought of a plan. "Really...a sword? I thought the black rider who commanded the Darkening would use the Memory Stone at the least."

He narrowed his eyes and his stare swept up and down over me. He put up a hand to touch the green jewel that hung from a chain around his neck. "So you know of the Memory Stone— how...interesting?"

I wet my lips. "I know more—I know that the three stones bring great power."

"Power? They do more than that, my little Flamma girl. But what I want is the one stone—the Dragon Stone, for that will give me use of all the stones together. I will be immortal—invincible. I will control the world." He smiled. "As to the Memory Stone, I have an army of slaves to do my bidding. Spending any more of my concentration on two children is not worth my time."

So it is difficult to bend another to your will? I thought of the old man. He'd been able to shake off the spell. Perhaps because he had Flamma blood in him, or perhaps because one of his kin had been a Dragon Rider...or perhaps just because this black rider was overextended. The gypsy stories had said the Dragon Riders could defeat the Darkening. There had to be a way I could use that to my advantage, along with Seb's Dragon Affinity.

I tried to reach out to Kalax, to poke her so she would poke at Seb. It seemed to work, for Seb blinked suddenly and seemed to come back to his old self. But Wulfric leapt forward at Seb, swinging his studded mace. Seb darted to one side and the mace crashed down on a rock pillar, shattering the top.

I turned. Lord Vincent strode toward me, his blade glittering in the torchlight. He lurched, aiming his sword at my heart.

Swinging up my sword, I managing to parry the blow and returned one. Lord Vincent parried my wild swing with ease. I stepped to the side, putting a stone pillar between us. I couldn't beat such a tall man with my strength and anger. I needed something more.

Beside me, I heard a grunt. I glanced at Seb and saw him block another blow from Wulfric, then ramming forward with the butt of his sword at the warrior's head. Light flashed and I turned. Lord Vincent's blade snickered toward me.

We swapped blows, our swords ringing. Breathing hard already, sweat dripping into my eyes, I had to yield ground. Lord Vincent's mouth curved, and I had the sense he was playing with me. He had the longer reach and the greater strength. I had...I had my connection with Kalax and Seb.

I couldn't do this on my own—I needed them. I needed a moment's distraction and help, and so I reached out to Kalax, hoping she would hear.

Need help. A roar...something.

From across the cavern, Seb gave a roar—and I heard the distant echo from above from Kalax. They'd heard me.

For an instant, Lord Vincent hesitated—he'd heard Kalax, but he wasn't sure what to make of the roar.

I reacted at once, spinning into a turn and extending my arm and sword. The blade skittered across my opponent's chest, scoring his armor and severing the silver chain that held the green, egg-shaped stone.

Vincent stumbled backwards. I seized the Memory Stone from the ground. It burned in my hand, seared my fingers, and for an instant the world blurred around me. It seemed as if I saw everything—armies gathering, the world through the eyes of black dragons. Like in my dreams, darkness swallowed me, held me fast. I was lost in it.

Beside me, Seb butted Wulfric with his body, pushing him so Wulfric's unprotected head thudded into a rocky outcrop. He fell to the floor.

I watched, held fast by the stone for an instant as Lord Vincent stood—right behind Seb, that narrow, pale face pulled into a snarl. The darkness held me—just like my nightmares of old. I was losing myself in it. But within the darkness, a light gleamed. Kalax's thoughts flew to me—her worry for us, her need to help.

Need to help, I thought. And I needed to be the Dragon Rider I've always wanted to be, no matter what it cost me.

With a cry, I pushed back against the tug of the Memory Stone. I was a Flamma—a Dragon Rider. I had the blood of centuries of Dragon Riders within me. I pushed Seb away. Lifting my sword, I turned, but not quick enough. The cold storm that was Lord Vincent's long blade slid through my armor into my heart. Pain swept into me, along with darkness—darkness, vast and final as my dreams had always foretold.

CHAPTER 29

AFTERMATH

I knew the instant Thea cut the stone from around Lord Vincent's neck. A wave of emotions exploded into me, making me stagger. It was as if all the controlled thoughts and feelings of the people and the dragons held by the stone's magic were freed. A physical gale buffeted me and for an instant the world was nothing but the thoughts of others.

Fear. Relief. Confusion. All the dragons—wild blacks and our dragons, too—gave a cry, as if suddenly aware of the change in the Memory Stone. The black dragons were no longer connected to Lord Vincent. For an instant, I could see the world through their eyes as they hissed at each other and realized they were free again. They rose up to flee in all directions, snapping and darting away. They had no desire to fight—they wanted to head back to their homes in the wild.

The people, too. I couldn't feel them individually, but I could see through the eyes of the dragons the people that had been enslaved by the Memory Stone were waking. They stumbled and dropped their weapons and some sat down again, holding their heads. The spell was broken.

Blinking, I used the emotions washing over me and slammed into Wulfric, thumping him hard against the stone. He slumped. I spun, needing my own thoughts, not those of a thousand dragons, but the dragons' fury held me. Thea slammed into me, knocking me aside. She turned, and a sudden look of shock spread over her face. Lord Vincent stepped back, pulling his blade from her—the blow had been meant for me. His sword had gone right through her armor with a killing blow.

With a cry, I let the dragon fury take over. I swung blindly, lashing out, spinning, turning, kicking, fighting with everything as a dragon might. The black form before me gave way, falling back as I slashed and hacked at him, cutting, crying out, letting the emotions inside me pour into action.

He lurched back, his sword clanking to the floor, clutching at his arm that I'd slashed. With a snarl, he fled.

Spent, the emotions drained out of me, I let my sword fall as well. I knew he must have felt the change as I did—that his plans were ended.

Heart pounding, head aching, I staggered back to Thea. Blood pooled around her. In her hand, she still clutched the Memory Stone. She had taken the blow meant for me. I tried to remember what to do about wounds. I tore my tunic sleeves off to stop the blood, but it soaked all too fast. Breaths rattled from Thea's mouth, pained, small ones, tinged by pink that slipped from her lips. I cradled her in my arms, my hands slick with blood as tears ran down my cheeks. She was dying. I knew it. I could feel her life leaking away. I felt desolate...destroyed.

Somewhere outside, I could feel Kalax howling, echoing my boundless grief.

I couldn't leave Thea in the darkness. Picking her up, I left our swords. She still held the Memory Stone clutched in one hand and I left it with her. I staggered out of one cavern, into the next, and then into the mine. I lost track of time, but I followed Kalax's thoughts—she guided me back to clean air and to a world where the sun was just coming up.

There, outside the mines, I slumped to the ground, without an ounce more energy to give. I couldn't tell if Thea still breathed, but when I touched her neck, I thought…I hoped I felt a faint fluttering.

Footsteps sounded behind me, hard rapping boots on the ground. I didn't know if it was Lord Vincent returning to kill me. I didn't care, except if it was him I would kill him with my hands. I could feel the rumble of Kalax nearby.

Dragons come.

I looked up to see the sky fill with Dragon Riders. They set up a guard, and two dragons landed near Kalax. I heard the fall of boots and then Commander Hegarty's deep voice sounded as he shouted my name. I looked up at the grim face of the commander, unable to smile or speak. I could only look back down at Thea.

"I know, lad, I know." He pulled at my shoulders to get me to stand and away from Thea.

"Can't leave her," I muttered, my voice croaking.

"You have to, Seb. You have to. Come on, lad. We've little enough time left. I only hope we found you before it's too late."

He dragged me up and away. My hand fisted, and then he reached into a leather satchel sung over his shoulders and pulled out a deep, white stone shaped like an egg.

"A dragon stone?" I whispered.

Commander Hegarty nodded. "Aye, the Healing Stone. It may be able to bring Agathea back, if we act quickly." He pulled aside the blood-soaked cloth from Thea's wound and held the stone over the bloody gash. A white radiance seemed to spill from the stone, falling into Thea like sunlight. I could feel a warm tingle from the stone, as if it was touching me…as if it was connected to every living thing and was using life to save a life.

The ugly gash on Thea's chest knitted itself together. She gave a sudden gasp and a cough. Her chest convulsed and she rolled onto her side, coughing and wheezing. I grabbed for her shoulders and held her.

"Water," she whispered. The commander slipped the stone back into his satchel and offered up a water skin. I touched a shaking hand to Thea's chest—all signs of her wound were gone, except for the blood caked on her clothes and the gash left on her armor. Commander Hegarty put a hand on her shoulder. "You'll feel terrible for some time, yet. The Healing Stone got to you just in time. Any longer and you would have been gone. Now, we have to get you both out of here."

"How...?" Thea coughed. "How did you find us?"

I shook my head. That didn't matter. I waved at the commander's leather satchel. "How is it you have one of the stones of power?"

He smoothed his mustache. "I've been the keeper of this stone for a long time now. Every Dragon Rider trusted with the secret must swear an oath, for the stones, they can do good, but they can also cause terrible destruction. Hardly anyone knows the stones exist, except in legend. I, for one, would like it to stay that way." Hegarty looked down to where the green Memory Stone sat on Thea's lap.

Gingerly, the commander pulled out a glove and slipped the Memory Stone into it. He tucked glove and stone into the neck of his leather jerkin, leaving it hidden by his armor. "As you two must know by now, these stones are too powerful for any one person. It is one of the tasks of the Dragon Riders to keep them safe, but we haven't always succeeded."

Thea sat up. I put a hand on her shoulder to keep her seated, and I looked up at the commander. "But the Dragon Stone...the one that controls all of them. Where is it?" I told him the story of what had happened inside the cavern—of Lord Vincent and the man named Wulfric, and how they'd been looking for the stones.

Commander Hegarty sighed and shook his head. "No. There is no one, great Dragon Stone. But there is an Armor Stone. There are three stones—we keep them in different places, sometimes within the academy, sometimes within dragon caves, and sometimes in simple huts. I've no idea how this Lord Vincent got the Memory Stone. We'll have to look in to that. But one great stone...that would be far too much power for anyone to hold."

Thea wiggled out from my hold and staggered to her feet. "Is that all the Darkening was the whole time—one man causing misery to others?

The commander shook his head. "I don't think we'll get any answers here. So let's get you two back to the Academy. There's a little matter to discuss of you not obeying orders."

*   *   *

The next few hours seemed a blur to me. Kalax greeted us both with a nudge of her head and an unhappy puff of smoke. I got the sense from her that if I ever left her behind like that again she was going to be more than unhappy with us. Thea actually hugged Kalax—or as much of Kalax's nose as she could. I asked Thea about that, but she only smiled and said, "We girls need a few secrets." We mounted and rode back to the Dragon Rider's camp. But we didn't stay.

The camp was already breaking up. Some Dragon Riders

were headed north on patrol, some were staying to help the town and its people recover, some were chasing black dragons back into the wild—it seemed a few of the blacks were interested in our trained dragons. We were due back at the academy, but the commander gave us a day there to recover.

Everyone seemed to want to ask us questions. We were led to tents, given water and basins to wash, fed and told to sleep.

I had no trouble obeying that order, but Thea left to go find her brothers. I fell asleep. I woke that evening and stepped outside, only to find Prince Justin's banner was flying in front of the tent. I'd slept like a prince! The prince's healers came to ask how I was doing and bring me more food and water.

Of the prince, however, I saw no sign. The healers told me Thea was with her brother, Reynalt, and the rest of the army had been ordered back to Torvald. It seemed the war had been called off. I wondered how much everyone knew, or had been told, of what had happened down in the mines. I also wondered where the Memory Stone had gone—did the commander still have it? I wanted to go find Thea, but I was still getting those headaches— not as bad as before, but bad enough to leave me happy to lie down and close my eyes.

I began to think the headaches had something to do with how the Memory Stone worked on someone like me who had the Dragon Affinity. The struggle and weight of all of those dragon's minds had almost left me thinking more like a dragon than a person, and I could see how someone might go mad with all those thoughts and feelings. I wondered if that was what happened to Lord Vincent—had he once been a Dragon Rider, maybe even the one charged with looking after the Memory Stone? Had he used the stone and had it driven him mad? I shuddered, closed my eyes and worked on better control of my thoughts. I finally got it so I could focus on just Kalax—she was relaxed and cavorting in the river a little way off, eating fish and washing her scales.

Black dragons smell bad, she thought at me. I almost laughed. I could feel her annoyance at how the black dragons had eaten most of the cattle and sheep around here, leaving no meat for anyone. Somehow the black dragons smelled different, and that was something I needed to think about. But that could wait until after we got back to Mount Hammal. I was tired enough that not even thoughts of being punished for disobeying the commander could keep me from sleep.

The next day I was given clean clothing—a tunic and breeches that almost fit, my old boots polished up, and a new leather jerkin. I just finished dressing when Thea walked into the tent with her brothers, Reynalt and Ryan.

"The hero awakens." Ryan's face split into a wide grin. He held up a basket. "We brought breakfast."

I pulled a face. "Ugh. I'm no hero, but you should have seen Thea in action." I dug into the basket, pulled out an apple that I threw to Thea. She caught it, winced a little and held her ribs. "Does it still hurt?" I asked.

"No. It's just…" Thea smiled. "Odd, like pins and needles or something. The commander says it's because it's new skin and flesh. It hasn't got used to the rest of me yet, I guess." Thea sat down, and I wanted to hear what she'd been doing. It seemed she'd been talking to everyone who mattered about what had happened—about Lord Vincent, and the Memory Stone, and how he'd been looking for the Dragon Stone. As we talked, I saw Reynalt and Ryan exchange a dark look as if they didn't like all this talk of magic stones.

I glanced at Reynalt, who was technically the highest ranking officer in the room. "When can we leave?"

He shared a glance with Ryan that I couldn't read and said, "We've gotten all the details about the mines that we can get. By the way, no one was there when we sent a squad inside. We're setting up a permanent guard here, however, just in case the Darkening tries anything like this again."

I wondered if they, too, were searching for whatever it was that this Lord Vincent had been after. I wasn't sure I believed that the Dragon Stone didn't exist—and a lightning-quick look flashed between the two brothers, telling me they weren't telling us everything. Thea either didn't notice the look or was too excited about the prospect of getting out of here. She turned to me and asked, "Are you fit to fly?"

"Uh, I guess so. Kalax is certainly itching to get away from this river valley."

"Good!" Thea smiled. "Eat up, and let's get out of here. I can't tell you how much I've been looking forward to getting the wind in my hair."

I could only agree, but I had to ask, "What do you think the commander will do to us for not staying at the academy?"

Thea shrugged. "Whatever it is, he'll have to make sure we keep flying. Kalax has been pretty insistent about that."

I stared at Thea. "You've been talking to Kalax?"

She grinned. "Well, not like you, but we communicate. How else do you think I keep an eye on how you're doing?" She slapped my shoulder. "Now, come on, eat up. We're heading home."

*   *   *

The Dragon Horn blew again, for the third and final time. This time I did not flinch or react with dread. This was not the signal for another test or another challenge, or even another grueling work day. Today was graduation and the deafening echoes of the Dragon Horns signaled the victory lap of honor.

I'd been waiting for the commander to look over and tell Thea and me we were out. Or that Instructor Mordecai would come over and grab us both and toss us out. Instead, nothing had been said. Finally, I couldn't stand it, and I leaned over and whispered to Thea, "When are we getting punished?"

She glanced at me, eyes wide. "I think you must be having problems with your memory."

"But Commander Hegarty said…"

"The commander spoke with Prince Justin—and with me and my family. Commander Hegarty couldn't remember ordering us to stay behind. So maybe he's the one having memory problems. Now will you shut up and enjoy the day—we're about to become Dragon Riders."

She grinned and faced front. I did the same, looking forward to where Merik and Varla stood side by side, looking resplendent in their Dragon Rider armor and horned helmets. Thea looked the same—we were all struggling to stay fierce, but we kept breaking out in grins like horned fools. The Dragon Academy had been opened and a wooden platform set up. The training area was crowded with instructors, families, nobles.

The high-pitched calls of ecstatic dragons filled the air as they flew past in perfect unison. First a triangular wedge, then two lines of dragons, all ridden by the best Dragon Riders. The crowd applauded as the final detachment of flying dragons separated from the group and flew downwards in lazy circles to the wooden platforms on the top of the walls. Our dragons were here to be celebrated, too.

"Your highnesses," Commander Hegarty's voice rang out, raising a goblet to the royal box where the king, queen and Prince Justin sat. "My lords and ladies, instructors, riders, families, friends; we hereby toast these new Dragon Riders. Long may they ride the air in defense of King Dorance and Torvald. May they have courage, honor and know the comradeship of the Dragon Academy."

A cheer rose from the crowd. People toasted and drank. I scanned the crowd and finally saw the banner for House of Flamma—a couple that must be Thea's father and mother stood, the man looking proud and the woman looking even more so. Thea finally had what she wanted—the respect of her parents. I glanced around and finally saw my father, step-mother and sister. For once Da looked like he was sober, and in a new jacket as well. He kept nudging the people around him and pointing to me. I looked away, my face hot.

Commander Hegarty waited for the crowd to settle, then lifted his voice again. "And I would like to say, my good assembled guests, this has been a trying time for Torvald, and for these new recruits in particular. The mining communities in the Leviathan Mountains were threatened and saved, but there may be dark days ahead. It is due to the courage of a few who risked all to whom we must give our greatest thanks. And I know you will join me in thanking these new riders, these navigators, protectors, and their dragons for standing fast against all dangers."

Another cheer rose from the crowd. I could feel my cheeks burning. Next to me, Thea nudged an elbow into my side. It was obvious that Commander Hegarty couldn't give us medals—the secret of the stones had to be kept. But I was happy to graduate with the other cadets—that was thanks enough.

"Now, will the newest recruits take the ancient oath of the Dragon Rider."

I opened my mouth, along with every Dragon Rider, to swear the oath:

By the First Dragon, I will always fly true,

To protect my partner, my dragon, and my king,

To help those who need my aid,

And to fight again the unjust, the unkind, and the enemies of Torvald

"Congratulations, cadets, you are now Dragon Riders. Come and receive your tokens," Commander Hegarty announced. The crowd cheered and tossed flowers into the air. One by one, the protector and navigator partners walked solemnly up to receive their tokens of office. In a few moments, it was our turn and we walked up to Commander Hegarty who pressed a pair of finely-tooled leather gloves of navigator ranking into my hands and the silver-gilt dagger of the protector into Thea's.

"Congratulations," the commander whispered as he gave us our tokens of office. "And I am happy you followed my orders to keep the academy safe—even if that meant leaving it without telling anyone. Just don't make it a habit." He winked at me. Those small words meant the world to me.

We continued up the stairs to the platforms, following the line of riders to their dragons. Kalax excitedly chirruped and put her large, red snout down to be scratched.

Both I and Thea reached a hand out to scratch Kalax's nose. I felt Thea's other hand slip into mine.

We might not know what was about to happen, what it meant now that the Darkening was back, and two of the three dragon stones were in the hands of the Dragon Riders. Lord Vincent was still out there, and still might be plotting against Torvald. But, whatever was on the horizon, we would face it together—the three of us.

End of 'Dragon Trials'

Book 1 of the Return of the Darkening

Dragon Legends, Return of the Darkening

Book Two is now available!

Read an exclusive excerpt below.

Thank you for purchasing 'Dragon Trials'

(Return of the Darkening Book One)

If you would like to hear more about what I am up to, or continue to follow the stories set in this world with these characters—then please sign up for my mailing list at

http://www.subscribepage.com/b7o3i0

You can also find me on me on

Facebook: www.facebook.com/AvaRichardsonBooks/

Homepage: www.AvaRichardsonBooks.com

Sneak Peek

Dragon Legends
(Return of the Darkening Book Two)

Blurb

Ever since scruffy Sebastian Smith and Lady Thea Flamma were paired as Dragon Riders, their lives have been forever changed. The unlikely duo forged an unbreakable bond, but now with dark stirrings in the south their bond will be put to the ultimate test.

Seb discovers Lord Vincent has returned and he wants to unleash an ancient evil that will destroy the lives of everyone in the kingdom – The Darkening. In order to defend the realm against unspeakable foes, Seb, Thea, and their shared dragon, Kalax, set out on an arduous journey to find the sacred Dragon Stones – before their dark power ends up in the wrong hands.

But to conquer an old enemy, Thea must find a way to overcome her own inner demons, and Seb has to muster the courage to become the brave leader his kingdom needs . . .

Start reading Dragon Legends today at
www.AvaRichardsonBooks.com

Dragon Legends
(Return of the Darkening Book Two)

Excerpt

The wind screamed past me, tugging at my armour and pulling at the goggles on my face as Kalax fell in a dive, straight for the bare earth.

"Seb!" Thea gasped the word and grabbed the back of my harness. I could feel tension and anxiety thrum through her body and into mine.

"Hold," I shouted with my mind and voice, leaning low over the long neck of our red dragon. Kalax's excitement, her eagerness for this fight, trickled up through the connection I had with her. But I had to concentrate. We had only one shot at this, and I had to be sure we didn't miss.

The ground grew larger, filling my sight. In a matter of seconds, the straight road that ran north to south from Torvald had turned from a faint, ochre line to a lane and I could make out the way markers on either side. The mounted figures beside the burning house looked like large dolls, but they glanced up and I could see their harsh faces.

"Now!" Kicking forward, I used the stirrups to activate the levers and pulleys that fed back to Thea.

Kalax roared, unfurling her wings in a sudden snap, catching the wind and sending a beat of air as powerful as a gale down on the bandits below. She roared again, the muscles of her wings and shoulders trembling under the strain of slowing her descent. I knew she could do this tricky maneuver—there were times when we were flying that Kalax and I became one body, one mind in flight.

The thunderclap of air swept in down at the bandits, startling their horses, sending two men sprawling to the ground and blowing apart bits of burning thatch before they could catch onto the rest of the structure. The smell of soot and smoke wafted up, as did the screams.

"Hyah!" Thea stood up in her saddle and fired down at the bandits. One arrow hit the side of the building, the other found its mark and the bandit who was attempting to mount his terrified steed fell.

"Up," I whispered to Kalax. Her excitement and thirst for the hunt bubbled up inside me. She could smell the terrified horses, and hadn't eaten anything all day except for a skinny old sheep this morning.

Hunt? The word appeared in my mind, flowing through the warm scales under my hands and blossoming with an accompanying desire for the thrill of the chase. Kalax was sharing her thoughts more and more with me now, rather than just listening to mine. Commander Hegarty had said it was because we were becoming more attuned to each other—but Merik, who I had told about it, thought it was a Dragon Affinity—an extra strong connection that I had with dragons.

No, I thought back at her. *Wait.*

Kalax was puzzled and I could sense her disappointment. But she rose into the air and circled.

"I've still got another shot," Thea shouted.

I glanced back at her. Some of her flame-red hair had come out of her helmet and she scowled, as fierce as the bandits. Two of the bandits below were carrying short crossbows—they could fire much quicker than Thea could draw her long bow. As the Navigator, it was my duty to choose the lines of attack and escape, and to keep Kalax out of danger. And Thea.

I didn't want to admit it, but I was afraid for her. The memory of her, lying on the floor of that cavern, blood seeping from the wound in her side as she lay dying, chased a shiver through me. I wasn't going to let that happen again.

The bandits below were screaming now, shouting to run even as another of them tried to call the others back. Three were fleeing on their mounts, headed south and into the wilds. *We'll leave them to the King's Patrol,* I thought, wheeling Kalax around in a wide arc to come back to the remaining four.

Small, black bolts sped past Kalax. One thudded into her scales, causing her to roar. I leaned to the side, wanting her to veer out of the way. The bolt had done her no harm, but I didn't want a lucky shot piercing her wing. My order confused Kalax for a second, making her spin in mid-air, before she turned and headed at the remaining bandits.

Thea shouted a war cry, and a flush of panic doused me in chill sweat. *What if they've had time to reload?*

But Kalax was fast. She fell on them, her forward claws seizing two bandits. She swooped past the half-demolished building and released them into the brambles. They'd be battered and bruised, and probably happy to give themselves up to anyone.

Standing in her stirrups, Thea shouted down at the bandit who seemed to be the leader. "Halt in the name of the king!"

One bandit turned and ran, leaving the last man—the biggest one—on his own against one of the kingdom's fiercest defenses—a Dragon Rider of Torvald. I wheeled Kalax around, preparing for another swoop. The man threw his sword onto the ground and raised his hands in the air.

With a triumphant roar, Kalax skimmed over his head a little lower than was necessary, knocking him flat. I had to grin. We had driven off the bandits and fulfilled our mission. And we had survived.

*   *   *

The King's Patrol arrived just in time to see Kalax land on the road, flattening the grass with the beat of her wings. I knew they had ridden out from the capital at the same time Commander Hegarty dispatched us, but no horse could match the speed of a dragon, especially not Kalax.

She was a red, meaning that some of the old bloodlines had resurfaced. Kalax had a long neck, tail and wings big enough to wrap around an entire house. She wasn't as sinuous as the blue dragons or as strong as the short-necked greens, or as fast as one of the wild blacks, but to me she was the perfect mix of all of their best skills. She had barbs that she could flare from around her face and along her tail if she ever needed to, and had teeth as long as my forearm.

At the moment, she was happily preening her thick wing like a bird, obviously happy with the day's work.

I swung off Kalax and glanced around.

The captain of the patrol looked to be a woman with a square jaw and fair hair scraped back into a thick braid. She wore leather armour, like most riders, but also wore a long sword and had a banner of the Middle Kingdom fixed to her saddle. Her warhorse

293

was large dark grey, but seemed a little skittish, snorting as if it didn't trust Kalax.

Kalax huffed out a warm breath and the captain had to hang onto her mount.

She glanced at me and said, "Captain Lacee. This is the leader, huh?" She nodded to where her men were tying up the last bandit who'd surrendered.

Thea unclipped her harness and jumping down. "Three more are fleeing southwards."

"We'll get them, no fear. As for these, they'll be taken back to the city. A year and a day of working on the high pastures or something and they'll rethink a career of theft."

Thea shook her head, crossed her arms and faced the bandit. "You're lucky. My father, Lord Flamma, would have had you whipped and thrown into chains."

I winced at the comment. As much as Thea had changed, sometimes the fact that she was from a noble house still came out at the worst times. Oh, sure she knew which knives and spoons to use at dinner, or how to address a lord or a captain or an ambassador correctly, but she also could stick that upturned nose of hers in the air and act like a snob.

It was different for me.

The only time I'd ever had to address someone of rank had been to say 'sorry sir' for an order that was late. I'd come from the poorest part of Torvald, and becoming a navigator and partner to Agathea Flamma was something I still wondered at. There were times I thought I'd wake and find this was a dream—or a nightmare, for rumours of war were still as thick on the ground as fallen leaves in autumn.

Thea turned away from the bandit, but I kept staring at him.

I was no expert on bandits, but this lot didn't look the type to be out for an easy gold mark. Most bandits I'd ever seen looked a lot like the people I'd grown up with in Monger's Lane, with dirty, patched tunics and cloaks that could hide their faces. They'd pushed through hard times. These fellows looked more like warriors. They could afford crossbows and swords, and wore stiffened leather armour, dyed red. They also wore their hair in an unfamiliar fashion with a braid running the length of their scalps and either side shaved. Tattoos covered their arms and necks.

"Captain Lacee?" I asked. "Where would you say these bandits are from?"

The captain turned to look at the man and nodded. "From a long way off. Up from the Southern Reaches, maybe."

That was an awful long way away. The maps I'd seen at the academy had shown the Southern Reaches were weeks away by horseback, and days even by dragon. Due to recent troubles, that would also take them through hostile regions.

Why come all this way to burn down a few houses?

"Don't worry, lad. Just bandits." The captain signaled for her men to mount and move off. "We'll be sending a team down to deal with those that fled." She threw a quick salute, mounted and rode off.

Thea leaned against Kalax and I scratched below Kalax's jaw at the spot she liked itched. "Let's allow Kalax to get her breath before we return." Thea nodded, but she seemed to stare at the horizon, as if she saw something I couldn't make out.

She didn't say anything, so I headed over the where the bandits had dropped their weapons. The long sword and the crossbows were all well-made. I'd learned enough of a smith's work from my father to know when a weapon was a costly piece, and these were worth more than any bandit would have found in this small village.

Something didn't feel right. Glancing at the ground I saw a leather pouch that one of the bandits must have dropped. Opening it, I found a shark's tooth, a few gold marks and a few beads. Keepsakes of a man whose life was on the road?

"Hey!" Thea walked up to me. "What are you doing?"

"Look at these." I showed her the items from the pouch. "A shark's tooth means from the sea—or the coast at the very least."

She shrugged. "So? It's not where they came from that matters, it's that we finished the battle in what, two minutes? Come on, Seb, we've rested enough. And you're looking for more trouble where there's none to be found."

She headed back to Kalax and I put the items back in the pouch and left it by the half-ruined house.

The truth was, I was worried about trouble—and feared it would find us before we were ready to be found.

We had defeated Lord Vincent and the Darkening once—but it hadn't been a full victory. Lord Vincent managed to escape and the rumours of the Darkening—of villages where everyone forgot their lives and simply disappeared—were still surfacing.

That meant the Darkening was still out there, probably regrouping to come at us again. And we still had no real idea how to defeat the Darkening for good—or even if we could.

Get Dragon Legends today at

www.AvaRichardsonBooks.com

53307540R00170

Made in the USA
Middletown, DE
26 November 2017